He Stopped Loving Her Today

Kezel Romanoff and Jeff Grover

Published by Romanoff Publishing, 2020.

HE STOPPED LOVING HER TODAY

First edition. December 19, 2020.

Copyright © 2020 Kezel Romanoff and Jeff Grover.

ISBN: 979-8223062479

Written by Kezel Romanoff and Jeff Grover.

Chapter 1

Alone in his room, Jared ignored the driving rhythm of the music blaring from his stereo while he slowly slid his fingers along the outside of his body armor. Struggling to peel the vest off, he grimaced through the pain of what felt like a dozen sledgehammers pounding on his chest. Finally the vest lost its adhesion to his skin and slid off. Shaking, and covered in sweat, he turned to the mirror above his desk. "Oh, shit!" He stared at the bruise on his chest feeling faint as the words to the song echoed off the walls.

He groaned, "Thank God I had that damn vest on," as he gingerly touched the melon size patch of dark red flesh in the center of his chest. He picked up a washrag and a bottle of water from his desk. Swiping his arm across his brow before pouring some water on the rag, he then tried to clean the dirt and sweat from his wound. The dirt stuck to his chest and he doubled over screaming in pain, "Mother of God!"

Embedded in the middle of the blood-shot flesh was the bullet that broke through the armor plates in his vest. Unable to grip the piece of fragmented metal with his fingers, Jared looked around the room for something to grab hold of it with. Spying a pair of needle-nose pliers on the nightstand next to his roommate's bunk, he half-crawled, half-stumbled around the bed, and seized them.

Sitting on the edge of the bunk, shaking, he used both hands on the tool to grip the fragment of copper and tugged. It refused to come out. He squeezed the pliers tighter and jerked hard. "Mother fu—"

Jared screamed at the searing pain. "Oh God, come out!" The rough edges of the jagged metal tore at his flesh as he worked it lose from the bone.

His eyes burned from the sweat dripping off his brow. Blinking, he held the thumbnail-sized copper jacket up to the light until he could see it with his blurred vision. Satisfied he had it all, Jared wiped the tears from his eyes and threw everything on the desk.

Rising carefully from his bunk, he stood in front of the mirror and stared at the wound. Blood trickled down his chest. He tried wiping at it with the damp cloth. His hands trembled so hard he could barely hang onto the washcloth. Closing his eyes, Jared took a slow deep breath, then another.

When his muscles began to relax, he turned to his wall-locker and dug out the bottle of Irish whiskey he had smuggled into the country. Tilting his head back, he poured a quarter of the bottle's contents down his throat, and then dropped into the overstuffed chair beside his desk.

Jared sat in the chair staring at the pack of cigarettes on the desk. Then taking another swallow, he snatched one from the pack. Using both hands, he was barely able to hold the lighter still long enough to light it.

After several drags, he wiped at the trickling blood and winced from the pain each time. With anger and frustration, Jared threw the dirty cloth at the wall, then downed most of the whiskey that was left. He sat staring at the red streak on the wall pointing to the rag on the floor, as the emotions of losing another friend in battle raged within him.

Suddenly, he slammed his fist on the desk. The ashtray bounced off landing upside down on the floor. Wiping his nose with his bloody knuckles, he climbed up out of the chair and fell against the metal wall of his hooch. He punched it and demanded, "Why did Dave die and I didn't? Why is it always the ones who don't deserve it? How come I didn't get any shrapnel from the grenade, we were both behind the same rock..."

His throat swelled from his anger and he flopped onto his bunk, thinking about the mission he just returned from...

THUMP...THUMP...THUMP... the spinning of the aircraft's rotors, created a distinct sound that could be heard for miles. It was the part of every mission he hated, knowing that the Taliban loved the slow-moving airships.

These damn things, we're like flippin' ducks in a carnival shooting gallery, was all Jared could think about as he tried to control his claustrophobic anxiety. *Focus on the beach vacation coming up in Hawaii,* he kept telling himself as the platoon was airlifted to a hillside above the outskirts of a small village in Kandahar province.

Lieutenant Dave, the group's leader, glanced at Jared sitting next to him. Knowing about his disposition with choppers, Dave calmly bumped him and asked, "How long you been doing this?"

"Almost two years." Jared took a sip of water from his camelbak to wet his parched tongue. "I hate being in these things. You stand a higher chance of getting killed in a chopper than on the ground."

"Then why'd you come back for a second time?"

"I don't know," Jared said. He stood as the Chinook settled in the dirt and the ramp dropped. "Maybe it was for the adrenaline rush."

With his feet firmly on the ground, Jared took in the layout of the land, making mental notes of the vegetation on the steep mountainous terrain, along with the barren rocky ravines. Quickly, he laid out a route with Harry, the point-man.

Walking quietly through the scrub-brush along the ridgetop, they searched for hours, trying to find the ravine that villagers claimed contained an enemy ammo stash. Dave, on his first mission outside of a wheeled vehicle, broke the silence asking Jared, "You plan on re-upping for a third round when we get back or you going home?"

Jared stopped. With the binoculars around his neck, he scanned the opposite hillside of the narrow valley they were in. "I'll probably be the last one out of this godforsaken place." Gradually, he turned and glassed the few mud and tin huts at the bottom of the mountain, then muttered, "That is, unless a bullet hits the bone."

Hitting Dave on the shoulder with the back of his hand, Jared glanced up the hill then nodded to continue forward. They walked through a cluster of trees in silence. Harry froze at the edge of the cover. Everyone else stopped in their tracks and watched him. The point-man knelt beside a tree and raised his rifle slowly, putting its scope to his eye.

"Confirmed," Harry whispered into his radio microphone. "Taliban, fifty yards ahead."

Everyone dove for cover just as the sniper squeezed his trigger. Instantly the air was filled with lead going in all directions. Minutes later, the shooting became sporadic, then stopped. After a few moments of quiet, Jared whispered in his radio, "Everyone OK? Count off and location."

All fourteen platoon members answered, except Dave.

"Dave, you OK?" Jared whispered into the radio.

No response.

"Can anybody see Dave?"

"He's behind that rock twenty feet to your left," Ronnie replied.

"Damn, give me cover!" Jared yelled as he jumped up and ran towards Dave. Weaving around the few shrubs in his way, he could see the sniper's bullets ricocheting off the ground around him. The closer he got to the rock that Dave was behind, the closer the enemy's shots came to their mark. Able to finally dive behind the car-size boulder, Jared yelled at Dave as he gasped for breath. "Why the hell didn't you answer?"

Sitting on the ground, with his back propped against the rock, Dave struggled to tie a bandage on his bloody leg. He grabbed the shattered radio from its pocket in his vest and tossed it at Jared. "You think it's bad?"

"What, the radio or your leg?" Jared retorted as he peeked around the boulder and listened to Dave's futile attempts at tying the bandage in place. Satisfied they were safe for the moment, Jared leaned over and took a closer look at Dave's leg. "Nope, missed the bone."

Snorting at Dave's feeble attempt, he grabbed the strings and re-tied the knot.

"What's this thing of yours about the bone? Or should I ask which bone you're talking about?" Dave snickered as he adjusted the dressing.

Jared was about to answer when Kuester's voice came over his radio. "How's Dave?"

Peeking around the boulder again, Jared keyed his mic, "Took one in the leg... and his radio's busted too. Ronnie, get on the phone and call a medivac for Dave. Can anyone see if that sniper is still around?"

"I don't see a body," Kuester replied.

"That's a negative," Ben whispered.

"You see him, Harry?"

"I don't have a good view of his location. How about you, Smitty?"

Smitty offered up, "I think he's done pulled a sage rat and ran back into his hole."

Tuning out the chatter from the rest of the platoon, Jared started to answer Dave's question as he leaned further around the edge of the boulder. "Heard it in a song. Has to do with cheating the reaper... ." Still unable to get a good view, Jared rose up a little higher before finishing with, "Until a bullet hits the bone."

The words were barely out of his mouth when a bullet tagged him in the chest, throwing him backwards. Jared's helmet did little to protect his head from striking the rocks on the ground.

THE THUMPING OF THE rotors roused Jared from unconsciousness. Lying on his back, he opened his eyes and saw Ronnie sitting next to him with his head buried in his arms. It hurt to breathe, but he had to ask, "What happened?"

Ronnie wiped at the dirt on his face with his sleeve. Taking a deep breath through clenched teeth, he choked as he looked up at the chopper's roof. "After you went down, all hell broke loose. There were seven of them in the tree line above us... it was a trap." He wiped his eyes with the back of his hand. "We were able to get five of 'em. The last two fired a RPG, then ran.... Dave had crawled over to check on you—" Unable to finish, Ronnie bit his lip. Closing his eyes, he leaned his head back against the chopper wall.

"Dave didn't make it," Kuester finished for Ronnie. "The grenade hit a rock beside him and he took most of the blast."

Jared grabbed Ronnie's pant leg, making a fist as he choked back the bitterness of what he just heard. Dave was the fourth member of his team to die in the last six months. He was the newest man in the platoon, yet in thirty days he won everyone's respect as an officer and a friend.

Cursing quietly under his breath, Jared dropped back down slowly, sliding his hand across his body armor. As he reached its Velcro zipper, he noticed the porcelain plates in his vest were broken. Cursing again, he dropped his hand down onto the deck. Learning early in the war to shed his emotions of the death and destruction in Kandahar, he laid there listening to the rotors in an effort to drown out his thoughts of losing Dave.

But this time he couldn't.

With a soft bump the Chinook sat down on the landing pad and dropped its back door open. Before the ramp hit the dirt, medics jumped on board and started to triage the wounded. They carried the two severely injured members out and everyone else except Jared followed the medics down the ramp. After the cargo hold cleared out another soldier walked on board with a body bag and laid it on the deck next to the blanket covering Dave. He looked at Jared. "Would you mind helping me?"

Jared nodded and rose to his knees so as not to collapse onto his fallen comrade. He reached for Dave's knees. Grimacing through the searing pain in his chest, he fought to do his best for his friend, but it was too much. Screaming in pain, he let go of Dave and fell back against the bench.

"You OK?" the soldier asked.

Jared nodded.

"You don't look good, let me get a medic to help you."

Jared wrapped his arms around his chest as he coughed, "I'm OK. I'm just sore from falling on some rocks."

The soldier squatted next to him. "I still think you should get checked out."

"No!" He shoved the guy away. "Take care of Dave and leave me alone."

Struggling to stand, Jared got to his feet and walked down the ramp, across the LZ to a humvee that had just been unloaded by another platoon heading out.

Jumping into the passenger seat, Jared asked the driver, "Hey, can I get a ride back to Charlie Two of One Sixty-two?"

Chapter 2

Unable to hide the wound that Dave's death did to his soul, Jared rotated to Frankfurt, Germany, to finish the last two months of his enlistment before going home. After arriving in Frankfurt, he decided to muster out and live there, where big city life would keep his mind off the past more than going back to the small town where he grew up could.

Feeling safe walking down the German streets, he felt he didn't need to worry that the scruffy beggar squatting against the wall might have a bullet with his name written on it. Or that the empty car, parked next to a street-side cafe, was packed full of explosives.

Life in Frankfurt was great. The vast quantity of GIs and ex-pats living there made it easy to find others who shared the same experiences. Together they reveled in the lifestyle of a country where beer was the national beverage. Life was easy, compared to spending two years in a 'dry' country where alcohol was strictly forbidden.

Not long after his discharge, the local recruiter tracked down Jared sitting at a sidewalk cafe. The recruiter dropped into the opposite chair uninvited. "Hey, Jared, you are one difficult person to find." He stuck out his hand. "My name is Sergeant Jones. I hear you just came back—"

"No!" Jared looked at the guy in a button-up tan shirt and shook his head. "I have my Two-Fourteen. I'm done."

"From what I hear, you had a good time and kinda miss it."

Jared took a drag from his cigarette. "I don't miss the formations and the BS."

A waiter came over to the table. Jones glanced at Jared, "You want a refill?"

Jared nodded.

Jones looked up at the waiter. "Two coffees and two slices of toast."

"You don't listen, do you?" Jared flicked his ashes into the ashtray.

"It's my job to listen," Jones said as he shoved the ashtray to the side of the table. "It's also my job to see that you don't miss out on the offer of a lifetime. Twenty-five Gs."

Jared picked up his cup, swirled the coffee inside it a few times then sucked it down. "Tempting. But I'm done."

"Let me give you my card." Jones reached into his shirt pocket and pulled out his card. Sliding it across the table, he snapped the card's edge as he pulled his hand back. "If you pick it up, you can see everything I can get put into your contract."

Jared picked it up, glanced at it, and snorted, "You're full of it. You can't guarantee me any of these."

"As the Senior Retainment NCO in Frankfurt I have the ability to make offers the others can't. Like, I can get you any base assignment you want..." he hesitated as the waiter placed the toast and coffee on the table. "You want to go back to the states, not a problem. How about Korea?"

"You think I was flippin' born yesterday, don't you." Jared took a piece of toast and bit into it. "I don't need you to get those assignments. And I'm not going back in, I'm finished."

"OK, OK. Give me a break, it's my job to at least try." Shoving the second coffee over to Jared, he dumped several packages of sugar into his own. "So do you have a plan for your time here. I mean you do have a job lined up?"

"Nope, still have to get on the DOD website and see what there is." Jared picked up the cup in front of him and took a drink. Wrinkling his nose, he grabbed several packets of sugar and dumped them in the coffee. "Probably need to find another place to stay, too."

"I'm having a party at my place this weekend. The address is on my card." Jones pointed at his card still laying on the table. "Come on over. There'll be several of the locals there, not to mention my mother-in-law. Who I think still has a room to rent."

"OK, I'll see if my calendar is free that day." Picking up the card, he slipped it inside the cellophane on his pack of cigarettes. Then placing the pack on his phone, Jared grinned. "What da ya know, it says I'm free. Anything I need to bring?"

Jones brushed the crumbs from his hands. "Flowers." He laughed at the quizzical look on Jared's face. "It's a culture thing to bring flowers to the host. And, no, the bar is well stocked."

"Any particular kind?"

"Something colorful. My wife understands that Americans lack cultural etiquette." Jones stood up and tossed a half-dozen euro coins on the table. "Great! Then I'll see you Saturday around one."

ARRIVING AT THE PARTY, he was greeted by several of his drinking buddies. Fred threw his arm around Jared's shoulder and punched him in the ribs. "I heard you were coming. I didn't believe it at first."

Harvey held out a beer. "It's an open bar. I say we go for it."

"Business first, I came here to talk about a job and an apartment." Jared took the beer. "Then we'll drink all his booze."

Fred rolled his eyes at Harvey. "Yeah sure. Just don't take too long, cause me and Harv are already on a roll."

"Fine." Jared tipped up his bottle and emptied half of it. "So who are all these people?"

"See that couple over there?" Harvey pointed at a couple next to the couch in the center of the room. "She works in Finance and he works in Logistics."

Fred cut in, "I hear they have quite a racket going on."

"You say that about every DOD employee." Harvey took a drink, then pointed at a woman next to the potted fern. "She works in S-3 operations. I believe she manages the packages stores and NCO/EM clubs."

"I could go for that. Bartender and free booze." Jared pulled out a cigarette and lit it. "Then coffee in the morning with her."

"You're too late." Fred took a swig from his bottle. "She's married to him." He pointed at Sergeant Jones. "But her mother is single, from what I hear."

The three chuckled. Jared wiped his mouth and held up his bottle. "I'm on empty, it's time for a new one. Where's the bar?"

Harvey pointed to the sliding glass door that opened into the back yard. The three went out and sat at the picnic bench next to the cooler full of beer. After awhile, Jones came out and began to prep the barbecue. "How you guys doing? Have you met everyone yet, Jared?"

Jared belched as he set an empty bottle next to the half-dozen other empties on the table. "Not yet, Jonesy. I'm still kinda waiting to find out about that room first."

"Room? Oh yes." Jones stepped back and threw a match on the kerosene soaked briquettes. "She'll be here about the time the steaks are done." He looked at Fred and Harvey. "Everything going fine?"

Fred smiled and nodded.

Harvey swirled the beer in his bottle. "Could use some more beer. We're almost out."

"Coming right up." Jones put the cover on the grill. "You guys don't mind watching this while I go get it?"

"No problemo." The table shifted as Jared attempted to stand. "Whoa! Careful with the table there, guys."

Jones tapped the table as he eyed Fred. "There's a bottle of Jamieson's behind the ice bucket on the bar."

Fred nodded and handed Jared another beer from the ice chest.

Harvey got up. "Jamison's boilermakers. That sounds sweet." He went inside and brought the whiskey out. "Now to find the cups."

"Who needs cups?" Jared snatched the bottle and poured some in his mouth.

Harvey, winking at Fred, slammed a five dollar bill on the table. "Bet you can't do that again."

Jared picked up the bottle, chugged four hefty swallows, and slammed the bottle on the table. Covering his mouth, he belched. "Whoa, that is smooth."

He picked up his pack of cigarettes and fumbled with them trying to get one out. Finally putting one in his mouth, he slid his hand along the table reaching for his Zippo and knocked it over the edge. Snorting a kind of laugh, he gazed at Fred. "You got a light?"

Harvey put a piece of paper on the table and held out a pen as Fred lit Jared's cigarette. "Five bucks say you can't write your name."

Jared ripped the cigarette from his mouth as he swayed back and forth. "Gimme that pen." He scratched a big 'J' on the blank paper. In his effort to move the pen and finish his signature, he pulled the cover paper from Harvey's grip. Jared squinted at the document under it. "What's this?"

Fred shoved the wrinkled blank paper over the document. "The bet is, can you sign your name."

Jerking the papers from Fred's hand, Jared glared at the re-enlistment contract that had been hidden under the blank paper. He snarled, "Why you mother," as he jumped up and decked Fred.

Harvey swung his beer bottle hitting Jared in the shoulder.

Jared managed to get his arm around Harvey's neck before Jones got involved.

Chapter 3

With the smell of urine and stale beer burning his nostrils, Jared regained consciousness on a cold, stone floor. As he laid there, he massaged his head in an attempt to soothe the pain. Thirst, and the foul taste in his mouth, made him think of water.

He grimaced as he took a deep breath and rolled over to get up. Opening his eyes the acrid stench of urine burned his eyes as he realized his face was on a grating over the floor drain. Jared pushed up onto his knees in an effort to get away from it.

There was no bed, no toilet, no nothing in the cell, just a light in the ceiling and a faucet sticking out from the wall. He crawled to the spigot and turned it on. Hanging his face under the flow of water, he rinsed his mouth before taking a drink. Eyes still barely functioning, he gazed around, then unzipped his pants and peed himself as he passed out again with the water still running.

THE METAL DOOR OPENED slow enough to make a painful metallic squeal, rousing Jared back into consciousness. Cringing, he covered his ears and whispered, "Stop. Stop."

After the noise stopped he glanced over at the door. An elderly jailer with a wicked grin and a bushy, gray mustache stood in the doorway. "Is this really how you want to spend the rest of your life?" the jailer asked with a heavy German accent.

Jared didn't answer as he struggled to sit up against the wall.

The jailer motioned, and stepped back into the hallway. "Come. Pay your fine, then you can get something to eat."

Inching up the wall to his feet, Jared shielded his eyes from the light and staggered into the hall in time to see the jailer step into the doorway of an office and toss his keys on the desk while glancing back down the hall.

Jared followed. Stumbling through the door, he caught his balance on the edge of the desk. "How the hell did I get here?"

Without a word, the gray-haired man took a thick book from a bottom drawer and placed it on the desk. He smiled with the tip of his tongue stuck between his teeth as he opened the book. He kept his tongue there till he found the page he was looking for, then answered, "You don't know?"

Jared wagged his head.

Chuckling, the jailer looked at the book and began to thumb down the page. "Lets see...fifty-five Euros to start with." He reached into the drawer again and pulled out a citation form. "Umm...fighting a police officer...two hundred thirty-four Euros."

"What do you...ohh." Jared squeezed his head. "What do mean fighting with the police?"

The jailer scratched his nose as he wrote on the form. "It took five officers to put the cuffs on you. You're lucky they did before Herman showed up."

"I don't remember a thing."

"Assault...no injury," he licked his finger and turned the page, "with injury...four hundred thirty-four Euros." The jailer sat back after he wrote the last figure down. "Would you like me to go on, young man?"

"No, no. Wait, what assault?"

"You broke your comrade's jaw." He closed the book. "You must have had one terrible disagreement with him."

Jared cradled his head deeper in his arms. "I don't remember a thing."

"It's been a long time since I have seen where it took so many Polizei to restrain one GI." The old man chuckled, "But, it must have been about this." He slid the re-enlistment contract Jared had scribbled on across his desk.

Giving the form a fleeting glance, Jared gently rubbed his black-eye. "Sheesh, that explains everything." He patted his shirt pockets. Finding them empty, Jared looked at the smiling guard. "Do you have a cigarette I can have? I seemed to have lost mine."

"You are lucky no one is pressing charges," the jailer said as he retrieved a pack from the top drawer and tossed it on the desk. "So your total fine is seven hundred twenty-three Euros."

Jared stared at the pack as he picked them up. "These are mine."

"Can you pay the fine?"

"You were going to keep my cigarettes!"

The old man picked up his pen. "Cost of cleaning the cell...twenty-five Euros."

"Cleaning what?" Jared demanded.

"Make that fifty, and now we're at seven seventy-three."

Jared took two cigarettes and tossed the pack back across the desk. "My mistake. Thank you."

"Can you pay?"

Putting one behind his ear and the other in his mouth, he felt around his pants for his lighter. "Umm, you wouldn't have a light, would you?"

The jailer pulled a Zippo with etchings on its side from the drawer and held it out. "Can you pay?"

Jared sat there for a moment, hanging his head as he thought. Then rubbing his face with both hands, he nodded. "Yeah, it'll put a big dent in my bank account. Damn."

With a grin of approval, the jailer leaned back in his chair and snatched a large baggie from the cabinet behind him. He took a piece of paper from within the baggie and placed it in front of Jared. "Here, sign for your belongings. And how would you like to pay? Cash or card?"

Dumping the contents of the bag onto the desk, Jared fumbled with his wallet as he tried to dig his credit card out. He pulled the card free, and with a trembling hand, held it out to the jailer.

As the guard reached over the baggie to exchange the lighter for the plastic card, he spied Jared's necklace in the bag. "That's an interesting pendant, it looks like a spent bullet. Something special?"

Silently, Jared slipped the chain around his neck, then pulled open his shirt to show the old man his scar and whispered, "Afghanistan."

With a nod, the jailer handed back the card but refused to let go of it until he got Jared's attention. "Is this how you want to spend the rest of your life?" He asked again.

"What are you talking about?" Jared slipped his lighter in his pocket. "This was a one time thing."

"Don't kid yourself, son. It's not the wound here...," the jailer tapped his chest, "that is going to haunt you. But the one up here," he said as he tapped his forehead.

"I'm fine. It's something to remind me of..." he shoved his card in his wallet, "of my time in the service."

Folding his hands across his stomach, the old man ran his tongue around his teeth. "If you say so."

"I do say so." Jared rose to his feet. "I'm going to be alright. It was just a one time thing."

"You're welcome to come back anytime and talk about it." The jailer picked up the empty plastic bag. Folding it he added, "Without the police escort, that is."

With his stomach in knots and a craving for a cup of coffee, Jared blew off the offer and stepped into the hall. "No thanks, I'll be OK."

Outside the Police Station, Jared headed across the street to a small bakery. Wiping his hands on his shirt, he opened the door and stepped up to the counter. Unable to focus his eyes on the menu board, he went ahead and laid a five Euro note on the cashier's plate, then ordered a cup of coffee with sugar and a Kaiser roll.

As the waitress carried his coffee to the counter, she clamped a cloth over her nose. Hurriedly taking the note, she set his roll and change on the plate then backed away from him, pointing toward the door.

Reaching for the roll, Jared caught a whiff of himself. "Damn, the pigpens back home don't smell this bad."

Outside, sitting on the sidewalk against the bakery wall, he devoured the roll and sipped at the coffee. "Maybe the old jailer was right," he muttered as he took the cigarette from behind his ear and stuck it between his lips. "All I've been doing is drinking since I got out. Maybe Frankfurt is the wrong place for me." He swallowed the last of his coffee and set the cup by his feet. "Maybe I should go to... Amsterdam, or to, ...London?"

Deep in thought, he lit his cigarette and stared up into the clouds. As the sun peeked from behind the clouds, he closed his eyes. Moments later there was a soft plink sound by his feet. Picking up his cup, a one Euro coin was in it. "Huh?" He poured the coin into his hand. " OK, heads A-dam, tails London."

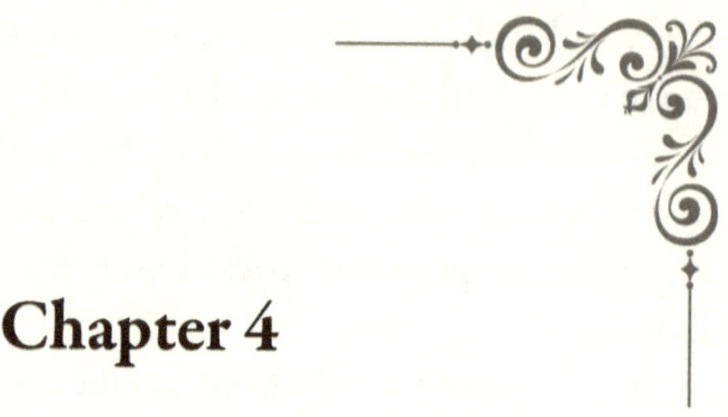

Chapter 4

The train pulled into Amsterdam Central train station. Outside the doors of the station, with the sun shining, Jared decided it was much too nice of a day to take a cab to his hotel. Passing by a tourist kiosk, he snagged one of the city maps and shoved the glossy paper in his coat pocket, then took off running to catch the crosswalk signal.

On the other side of the street, he shoved himself into the crowd on the island median. With his heels on the edge of the island, traffic rushed by behind him while a tram moved slowly around the curve in front of everyone. The clicking noise from the tram's wheels resonated in his ears. It had the same rhythm as that of a Chinook's rotor blades. The sound quickly sucked his thoughts back to Afghanistan. Wanting to move around in an effort to ease his anxiety, he couldn't. He was hemmed in. The dread of the chopper ride before each mission gnawed at his gut once more.

Finally, the tram stopped and the crowd surged across the street to the other side. With a sigh of relief, Jared followed. Only to realize the large pack on his back prevented him from slipping through the crowd. Instead, it made him captive, having to wait for the person in front of him to move before he could take a step. He soon found himself being herded against a building one moment, then into the doorway of a shop he had no desire to go into the next. The more he fought with the crowd, the more his claustrophobic sensation developed into a full blown panic attack. In a last ditch effort, Jared forced his back against a wall and lit a cigarette. The squeeze of tourists shied away as he stood there blowing smoke at them.

After he finished the cigarette, a college-age group of Brits and Swedes passed by. Many of them had large packs slung over their shoulders, too. Seeing their buoyancy, Jared became adamant he was not going to let his fears ruin the day. He stepped away from the wall and at first, just walked with the group. When he found out they all spoke English, he quickly joined in their chatter, making new friends.

Hours later the group found themselves meandering through a small square next to a wax museum. Their leader raised his voice, "the hostel where we are staying is just around the corner. We need to check in before going anywhere else."

The two girls standing next to Jared urged him to join them at the hostel. Rolling his eyes at the puppy dog looks they were giving him, he laughed, "I wish I could, but I've already paid for two nights at the Pension Valken."

"Please, please," they begged, giggling.

"Tell you what," he pulled out his phone, "I have nothing to do tomorrow. Give me your number and I'll come hang out with you guys. We can see the town together then."

After exchanging numbers, they parted ways and he drifted down the street alone. The long shadows on the sidewalk reminded him he hadn't eaten since breakfast. He searched in his pockets for the map while he walked. "Now where did I put that thing...?" His stomach growled for attention. "OK, OK. Food first, then the guest house."

Catching a delicious scent as it wafted along the canal, he rubbed his belly and mumbled, "you're in luck my friend, I smell something close by."

In the middle of the next block, he found a cafe with a few tables under an elm tree next to the water. Sliding into an empty chair, he dug out his map. "Now to do some research." He studied the glossy paper. No matter how hard he looked at it, he couldn't find the hotel.

"Dang it. I shoulda picked a different map up from the reservation office instead of this thing."

Jared took out his phone, looking up the hotel's address, he held the phone over the map in an effort to compare them. Faintly, he heard a voice in the background as he stared at the map and chose to ignore what he perceived to be the ringing in his ears.

The waitress spoke again, this time slightly louder. "Hello."

Jared looked up. The voice, wore a white blouse, blue jeans, and long, black, straight hair. "Sorry, I was lost in thought," he said, dropping his phone as soon as he saw her.

"American, yes?" she asked as she rifled through the large pocket of her apron.

"Yes, but—"

She pulled out a small menu. Placing it on the table next to his arm, she left without a word, going back into the cafe.

The menu, in English, surprised him. With a quick scan, Jared decided what he wanted then looked around to signal her he was ready. Not seeing the waitress, he went back to his map and continued his search for the hotel.

He found the cafe he was sitting at.

The reservation slip in his hand said the hotel was located at number 49 on Canal DeBeersstaat. He looked over at the cafe entrance. It had a 49 above its door. The sign on the bridge over the canal, said it was the Debeers Canal. Frustrated with not being able to read a simple tourist map, Jared tossed it on the table and took out his cigarettes. His stomach protested out loud. Tossing the pack on the table, Jared looked around for the waitress with the angelic voice.

She was nowhere.

He leaned back in his chair and glanced once more at the door of the cafe just in time to see her come out headed his way.

Finally, I was beginning to wonder. He slid forward and picked up the menu.

She stopped at the table next to him and took their order first.

He watched her and waited.

She looked over her pad at him after she finished scribbling their order. As his eyes locked on hers, Jared raised his index finger and smiled.

She raised her eyebrows, nodded, and then disappeared back into the cafe.

He shook his head with disbelief, *I got better service in a Taliban restaurant than I'm getting here.*

Rising to his feet and lighting a cigarette, he stuffed the pack in his coat pocket, and reached for his phone and the map. After shoving them together in another pocket, he grabbed his backpack. Bumping into someone as he turned to leave, the waitress stood in his path with a cup of coffee and a ham sandwich on her tray.

Embarrassed, Jared dropped the backpack and sat. "How did you know? I mean, thank you."

"Een." She held up her index finger.

Jared picked up the sandwich and studied it for a moment before shoving it into his mouth.

She fanned herself with the menu and watched him. Shaking her head slowly, she turned and walked away. At the cafe door, she glanced at him once more before stepping inside.

The warmth of embarrassment left his face as he scarfed down the sandwich, trying to satisfy his stomach. Finishing the first half, he picked up the sugar packet from the tray and dumped it into his coffee. Taking a sip, he watched a small group of tourists pass by. "This might be the place, it's a little more laid back than Frankfurt," he whispered into his cup.

He attacked the second half of the sandwich at a much slower pace while watching the waitress do her job. With the last bite in his hand, she walked by and set another cup of coffee on his table.

Surprised, Jared blurted out, "Thank you."

The breeze flowing along the canal turned chilly by the time he finished the second coffee. The chill caused him to shudder, reminding him he needed to find his hotel. Pulling two crumpled euro bills out of his pocket, he wedged one under the cup without looking at it.

Rising to his feet, he quickly caught a whiff of a familiar pungent odor. His soldier's instinct kicked in and he started to scan the surroundings. A momentary flashback of a firefight in Kandahar caused him to look with deep concentration at each window down the street.

The clank of dishes and the rattle of chairs followed by an, "Ahem," seized his attention. The waitress stood beside him, holding out a five euro note.

Distracted by her beautiful smile, Jared stood looking at her in a total loss as to what she wanted.

She raised her eyebrows and waved the bill in her hand.

He looked down at his hand and saw the crumpled ten euros still between his fingers. "Oh, sorry, I didn't mean..." he held out the larger bill.

She took them both and gave him his change.

He looked at the coins in his hand as she picked up the tray with his dishes. Jared dropped the coins on it. "Thank you. It was the best thing I've had to eat all day."

She winked and started to walk away.

"Uhm, uhm..." Jared struggled to find the right words in Dutch to ask her for directions. Finally he yelled out, "Wait."

She calmly looked over her shoulder at him. "Yes?"

He held up the map. Again, he fumbled for words as his mind went blank. All he could do was point at his map.

She set the tray on a table. Smiling, she walked over to him, took the map from his hands, and looked at the address written on it. Shaking her head, she turned it upside-down and handed it back.

Jared looked at the map. "What?"

"There." She pointed across the canal.

He looked in the direction she pointed and saw the small sign, *Pension Valken,* hidden by the Elm trees along the canal.

Chapter 5

Waking up with the sun shining on his face, Jared rolled out of bed and stood next to his fifth floor window looking down on the canal. Curious as to what the Amsterdam skyline looked like, he opened the window and leaned out. "It's a good thing I didn't have any expectations, but at least the sun is shining," he muttered. He closed the window and started humming John Denver's, *Sunshine on my shoulders*. With it stuck in his head, he turned away and slipped on his pants. Grabbing a cigarette, he lit it and walked over to the window while buttoning his shirt. This time he noticed he could see the table where he had sat the evening before. The image of that cute waitress knocked Denver's song from his thoughts and at the same time the smoke from his cigarette curled upward, burning his nose. He shook the smoke and the thought of her out of his head. "Stay focused, my man. You're going to try and meet up with those two Brits." Snubbing the cigarette out he turned toward the door. "And before that, it's breakfast."

He jumped down the stairs two at a time to the second floor, and walked through the arched doorway of the breakfast room. The only empty table left was on the far side of the crowded room. Jared twisted and turned to avoid the other guests' elbows as he inched his way toward the table.

At the table, he shook his fist and whispered, "Yeah, not one bump." His excitement faded as he sat down and looked toward the kitchen, only to realize it was self-serve. Rolling his eyes, he was about to get up when the landlord finished his waltz between the tables with two cups and a coffee carafe. "Koffee? Ja?"

"Yes! Please."

The proprietor dropped into the chair across the table from Jared and filled both cups. "You are American, yes?"

Jared nodded.

"May I offer you some advice to make your stay...shall I say, pleasant?"

Jared picked up his cup with both hands and held it under his nose while he eyed the owner with a graying ponytail, who he guessed to be about forty. After taking a sip, he set his cup down. "Sure, why not?"

The owner lowered his cup and leaned forward. "If you came to visit the coffeehouses, keep an eye out for the pickpockets just outside their doors."

"Don't worry, I didn't come here to smoke pot." Jared poured some sugar into his coffee. "I did come here for therapy. Just not that kind," he admitted as he looked around for something to stir with.

Producing a spoon from his apron, the owner slid it across the table. "The same goes for those ladies. Some have three hands."

"I'll remember that," Jared babbled as he took out a cigarette. Tapping the filter on the table, he joked, "How about the diamond market, is that safe?"

"Don't light that in here, please." The landlord sat back and crossed his legs, giving Jared a serious look. "I don't know, but I can find out for you."

Jared put the cigarette behind his ear and leaned forward, whispering, "No, no, that's OK. What I really want to know is, where I can find a job."

"Uhmm..." the landlord picked up his coffee. "You and every other émigré in this city." Scratching his eye, then watching some of the guests as they left the room, he asked, "How well do you speak Dutch?"

"None. I mean, I can speak some German." The coffee caused Jared's stomach to rumble loudly. He rubbed his belly as he looked over at the buffet table and exclaimed, "What I had in mind was, maybe, like just a few hours a week so I could learn the language, shall we say... pleasantly."

As he picked up the carafe and glanced into it, the landlord took a long deep breath. "My friend, I wish I could help you, but as they say in your country, you are up a creek without an oar."

"Paddle."

"What?"

"It's, up a creek without a paddle."

"Oh." The owner stood and poured what was left in the carafe into Jared's cup. He glanced around the now empty dining room, then wiped at some coffee on the table. "Go ask the ladies, sometimes they will hire someone to pass out advertisement cards."

Jared snickered at the thought of a prostitute paying him as he watched the proprietor walk back toward the kitchen. Turning, the owner warned, "Oh, and be careful of the Roma."

Jared stood, drained the last of the coffee from his cup, then made his way to the buffet bar, where he shoved an apple in his coat pocket and stuffed the last bagel-egg biscuit in his mouth. Ripping a bite off, he headed for the door.

Out on the street, habits that were ingrained from several years of deployment made him stop and recon his position. He made mental notes to the safety of his being in the open. Then he took in landmarks so he could find his way back among all the look-alike buildings in the neighborhood.

Suddenly, a movement across the canal caught his attention. It was the cute waitress he had met the day before, setting up tables at the cafe. He waved to her, then headed in the direction of the hostel the Brits were staying in.

It didn't take long on the narrow sidewalks before he was caught behind a large group of tourists in his path. Trying to be polite and not push his way through them, Jared ducked into an alley toward the next street over. That street twisted off in a different direction and quickly dead-ended. With nowhere else to go, he backtracked to a small bridge over yet another canal and went through another narrow pedestrian alley.

At the end of the alley, he stepped out onto a wide sidewalk, filled with more slow moving tourists. Jared pulled up a map on his cell phone showing another path between buildings, about a hundred feet in front of him.

Frustrated when it wasn't there, he put a cigarette in his mouth. Bowing his head against a lite breeze in his attempt to light it, he caught sight of the alley just a few yards away. He shoved his lighter in his pocket and pulled out the paper tourist map as he stepped into the dark, covered pathway.

Walking in the dim light, he tried to read the black and white map while the smoke from his cigarette burned his eyes. Cocking his head to the side to avoid the smoke, he held the paper out at arms length and stepped out into the next street without looking.

Blindsided by a bicycle, Jared twirled, dancing to keep his balance, all the while grasping for anything to keep him from falling. He latched onto a second bicyclist's jacket just as he stubbed his toe on one of the cobblestone pavers, slamming both of them into the side of a parked car.

With a groan, Jared clambered to his feet and offered a hand to the bicyclist. "Hey buddy, I'm really sorry."

The cyclist, tangled up with his bike, brushed Jared's hand aside and made his own effort to get up. Unable to get his footing, he finally gripped Jared's hand and rose up enough to lean against the car. Taking several deep breaths, the biker massaged his shoulder as he rotated his head back and forth.

Jared coughed, "You OK?"

The bicyclist stood up and glared at Jared while he tugged his jacket into place. Jared offered him another, "Hey man, I'm really sorry."

Ignoring the apologies, the cyclist reached for his bike.

Jared stepped back out of his way. "Hey, come on...let me get you something, a coffee, water, or a croissant."

The guy looked his bike over. Then he slowly looked down the street and gestured in approval, "There."

Jared followed him down the street, where the guy chained his bicycle to a rack and commanded, "Come."

They walked in silence to the end of the next block and stopped at the door to a coffeehouse with its name emblazoned on a green cross in the big display window. Entering, Jared noticed ashtrays on all the bare wooden tables. Relaxing a little, he pulled out a cigarette and lit it as they sit down.

Reaching across the table, he offered his hand. "My name is Jared. I really didn't mean to pull you down."

"Hans." The cyclist grasped Jared's hand and shook it. "I'm OK."

"Hans. OK." Jared picked up a menu that lay on the table. "Let me make it up to you. Order anything you want. It's on me." Glancing at the menu, he saw it was in Dutch. Tossing it back onto the table he looked at Hans with a bit of curiosity. "You speak English?"

"Yes. My English...OK," Hans replied with a distinct accent. "Which way do you like smoke? I mean, do you have preference?"

"I'm a Marlboro man myself." Jared pointed to his pack on the table. "You're welcome to one if you'd like."

Hans shook his head.

Looking around the coffeehouse, Jared noticed the group occupying another table were sharing a hookah pipe. "But, umm...you go right ahead and get what you want. It's the least I can do for knocking you off your bike."

Hans turned in his chair and said something in Dutch to the person behind the counter. The waitress came over and placed two coffees and four muffins on the table, then waited as Hans held up the menu and pointed at it as they exchanged a few words.

Jared reached over and took one of the cups. He stirred in some sugar as the waitress nodded and left. Immediately, he stopped and stared at his coffee. Setting the spoon on the saucer, he glanced at Hans, then down at his coffee. Holding the cup up to his nose, he inhaled the aroma, thinking for a moment that maybe—, he shook his head and took a sip.

The waitress returned minutes later placing a small plastic canister and a package of rolling papers on the table. Hans fastidiously rolled a joint while Jared alternated between watching him and staring at the muffins. When Hans finished, Jared asked, "Is there any...cannabis in the muffins?"

Not paying attention, Hans held up the joint looking at it. When he saw Jared's face, he laughed, "No, comrade, there is no hashish in pastry."

With relief, Jared snatched one, ripped it in two, and shoved half into his mouth. He swallowed it without chewing. Taking a sip of coffee and leaning back in his chair, he watched Hans light the joint and hold his breath. As he nibbled on the other half, he wondered what to think about his new acquaintance. "What kind of a job," Jared waved the muffin in his hand to emphasize his words, "or work, do you do, where you can smoke that stuff?"

Hans took a drink of coffee and twisted in his chair, stretching the muscles in his back. "I work canal boat. No work today. Is day off." He put the joint in the ashtray and took one of the muffins. Swallowing a bite, he picked up the joint and took another puff. Exhaling, he offered, "if you like tour of city, give me call."

Still puzzled, Jared nodded. "Sure."

Hans pulled a card from his coat pocket and laid it on the table. "Tonight I play music in club." As he tossed another bite in his mouth, Hans's face went blank. "Club? Oh no! Late for practice." Jumping to his feet, he grabbed the cannabis container. "Thank you comrade." He snubbed out the joint and shoved it in the canister. Then he leaned over and slid the business card in front of Jared. "Call me."

Lost as to what Hans's rush was, Jared watched him disappear out the door. Unaware of the smoke in the room getting thicker, he finished the rest of his coffee, along with the last muffin. Uncertain of what to do next, he stared out the window. Slowly, he picked up Hans's card and put it in his back pocket. "Awe, what the hell, may as well get lost in town."

Chapter 6

Late in the afternoon and burned out from walking around Amsterdam, Jared glanced at his phone. "Almost time for dinner," he muttered, and headed back toward the hotel. Reading restaurant menus posted outside their doors, and choking on their outlandish prices, he wondered if he could afford something other than pizza or the golden arches.

Crossing a dozens bridges on his route, all the canals that looked alike. Lost, he stopped on the latest and looked up the canal. He saw the cafe by his hotel where he had eaten the day before. Excited, Jared left the bridge and made his way toward the cafe's outside tables. As he walked toward the tables, he kept an eye on the cafe's entrance to see if *she* was working.

With no one else close by, he pulled a chair out from a table. The steel feet made a loud scraping noise. He dropped into the chair and put his boots on the seat of the chair across from him.

Instantly from behind him came a snippy command. "Please remove your feet."

"And who's gunna make me?"

"You Americans are all the same. Arrogant and self-centered. If you do not remove your feet, I will send for the cook."

Jared put his feet on the ground and leaned backward to see who was speaking to him. It was *her*.

Flush with embarrassment, Jared sat up straight. "Oh, you do speak English. I mean...I'm sorry."

"Of course I can speak English." She sorted through her menus and held out the one printed in English. "Would you like this, or do you know what you want?"

"Umm, yes, I do." He wiped his hands on his pants then took the menu. "I didn't mean to be rude, and it's Jared."

"That's not on the menu." She picked up three empty glasses from another table. "Do you know what you want?"

He glanced at the menu. "Aaa...a bowl of soup. With a sandwich."

She dropped her arms, holding the glasses down by her side. "You want a sandwich and a bowl of what?"

"Sorry, bean soup."

"OK." She turned and left.

Jared stared at her as she walked away. "Wait. What's your name?"

"Why? You'll be gone in a day or two," she said without breaking stride.

He pulled out a cigarette and sat back. *Damn, that went well. Proves I'm definitely no James Bond with women, that's for sure.*

He tapped the filter on the table and took in the surroundings. A couple next to the canal, got up and left their table. He stuck the unlit cigarette in his mouth and stood up to move over to the now empty table.

"Are you leaving?"

Surprised, Jared spun around and at the same time tried to catch the cigarette as it fell from his mouth. "Damn, you startled me. I mean... no. I'm moving over to that table by the canal."

She looked at the table he pointed to. "You didn't say what kind of sandwich you wanted."

"You didn't tell me your name." Jared grinned. He took a step forward. "What kind is there?"

She stepped back out of his way. "Roast beef, ham, egg."

"Roast beef."

She followed him. "Why should I?"

Jared stopped and looked at her. "Would you prefer that I snap my fingers and yell, hey you?"

"I won't answer to that."

He sat down at the new table. "What kind of soup did I ask for?"

She picked up the empty dishes left on the table and turned towards the cafe. "Angelina."

"What kind is that?"

She wagged her head. "My name."

With a deep breathe and a sigh, Jared took his Zippo from his shirt pocket and lit the cigarette hanging from his mouth as he watched her walk across the patio into the cafe. Snapping the lid of the lighter closed, the etching on its side grabbed his attention. It was a picture of a combat infantry badge. He turned it over. Carved into the Zippo's chrome, was the name of his unit: Charlie Company 3/162 1st INF.

Jared stared at the words while his thumb gently rubbed the etching. Memories of people from the not too distant past, flooded his thoughts. In a catatonic state reliving the war in Kandahar again, Jared was unaware the cigarette in his hand was now burning his fingers and that his food was being placed in front of him.

Angelina tried to get his attention, "Hello."

Jared didn't flinch.

Pulling a chair out across from him, she sat and asked, "I'm on break, do you mind if I share your table?"

He blinked, but didn't move.

Smelling his burning flesh, she poured water from her glass on the cigarette's ember.

His fingers wiggled while he stared straight ahead.

She tapped his soup bowl with a spoon. "Hello. It's getting cold."

Blinking his eyes, he snapped out of it. "Sorry. I...I—" Wincing at the pain, he flicked the cigarette from his hand onto the ground. Picking up the spoon, he held the cold metal to the burn on his finger.

Angelina looked at him as she stirred her coffee. "That's OK, my father went through the same thing."

"What kind is it?" he asked looking at the soup.

She sat back and smiled. "Onion. Goes with the roast beef."

Placidly, he moved the utensil through the soup several times. "It looks like bullion, too bad it's not in a cup." His eyes fluttered a few more times before he laid the spoon down. Raising the bowl to his lips, he took a sip. "Umm, good choice."

"Not only are you arrogant," Angelina snickered, "but you're also ill-mannered."

"That's why I didn't go home." He sat the bowl down and picked up half of the sandwich. He grinned as he pointed at her. "I figured I could teach you Europeans some manners."

She covered her mouth with the back of her hand to keep from spitting out her coffee as she giggled. "What could you teach us?"

Jared took a bite, then looked up into the crown of the elm tree next to them. "Uhmm, let's see. How to dance?"

Squinting at him, Angelina set her cup down and stared at him. "Are you serious?"

Jared raised his eyebrows. "Yeah."

Laughing, she nearly fell from her chair. After a few minutes, Angelina regained her composure and wiped her eyes. "What do you know about dancing?"

"Hey, I've been to my share of clubs in Frankfurt."

"Clubs, mmm." She took a pen and a notepad from her apron. "Dancing, huh?" Angelina looked at him, then wrote an address on the paper. As she rose to her feet, she slid the paper in front of him. "If you think you can show me how to dance, I will be here at ten p.m. tonight."

She picked up their dirty dishes and stood there for a moment studying his face. When he took another bite and didn't pick up the note, she raised her eyebrows. "I have to go."

Angelina was across the wide patio, almost to the cafe door by, the time Jared picked up the paper. He raised his voice and asked, "Is this a date?"

With a seductive look over her shoulder, the slender black-haired waitress smiled. "Show up and find out."

Chapter 7

The cab turned the corner and stopped. Jared looked above the different doors for the address Angelina had written down. The driver turned on the inside light, noticed Jared's bewildered look, and pointed to an unlit doorway in the corner of the building across the street. "There," he said.

Handing over the fare, Jared quickly copied the taxi's phone number into his cell phone.

As the cab pulled away, Jared took out a cigarette and put it in his mouth. He stared at the darkened doorway. *What is with these European clubs? They never have any signs. I've yet to see one that doesn't look like an abandoned building.*

He stood on the corner debating if she had gotten it right and that the darkened building really was the Club Madrid. "Well, the only way to find out is go knock on the door," he muttered and stepped off the curb.

A squeak from a car door a half-block down the lane stopped him. A couple stepped from their car and walked to the darkened entrance. The man pushed an intercom button while the woman kept an eye on Jared across the street smoking his cigarette. At the sound of the door unlocking, she stepped closer to her companion.

Guitar music drifted out of the open door into the night air. The man took a brief look over at Jared before following the woman inside and letting the door swing shut.

Jared walked over and looked at the intercom. Next to the button was the word, *Private*. "Great, twenty minutes early, and it's a member's only club," he muttered.

With nowhere to wait, he stepped around the corner from the door. As soon as his back touched the wall, a metallic tapping sound began to play with his attention. He looked up and down the street to see where the sound was coming from. A slinking shadow flirting among the parked cars hissed. Jared flicked his cigarette butt at it. "Go away, cat. You're messin' with my head."

The cat disappeared, along with the sound.

Jared looked at his phone. "Been here only ten minutes, damn! Oops, watch your mouth, boy. 'member, you're not out with the buds."

Pushing away from the wall, he walked around the corner to the next street. He stared into the dimly lit canyon between buildings. "Dang, there's no way I would drive in this place. Cars parked bumper to bumper. Bicycles chained to everything." He walked down the block to the next intersection. "This lane's not a foot wider than the cars. Absolutely not!"

Gazing in all four directions, all he could see were four-story houses made of concrete and not an inch between them. Continuing his circle around the block, he lit another cigarette.

At the next corner he stopped. *More of the same...and two women walking this way.*

Jared sandwiched himself between two cars in order to give them room to pass. The ladies, in brightly colored long dresses with shawls draped over their shoulders, smiled as they approached. Stopping beside him, they ardently inspected him like he were a thoroughbred horse for sale. The one with polka-dots on her dress purred, "Grrrr. What have we got here, Marta?"

"Sorry, ladies, I'm waiting for my date."

Marta, in a sky-blue dress, smirked, "What a shame, Sarina. He would look good on my arm."

She batted her eyelashes then smacked her lips as she blew him a kiss.

Giggling like a pair of school girls, the two walked on, arm in arm, to the club door.

"Must be the cologne I'm wearing." Jared laughed and tried to step from between the cars. "What the heck?" He looked down at his feet. One of his laces was tangled with a license plate. Reaching down to untangle it, a taxi drove by, missing his head by inches. The cab stopped in front of the club.

Its back door swung open and Angelina put a foot on the curb as she handed over her fare.

Jared jerked his foot free and hurried over to greet her. She was a stunning sight to behold as she stepped from the cab. Speechless, all he could do was stare.

"What do you think?" Angelina asked, as she brushed her very tight-fitting maroon blouse and layered long black skirt.

Jared blinked several times. "You look absolutely amazing."

"Thank you." She draped an elegant white lace mantilla over her shoulders, then pulled her long black hair out from under so that it hung freely down her back. "Been waiting long?"

"Uhm, no. Just got here a few minutes ago."

She grabbed his arm and nudged him toward the door. "Glad you came. I was betting you wouldn't show."

"What do you mean, not show?"

She pushed the button on the intercom. Then fluttering her lashes at him, she quipped, "That you would find an excuse not to come."

"I said I would," Jared winked and haughtily stuck his nose in the air, "to show you—"

The speaker hummed. Angelina leaned close to it. "Angelina Rozenska."

Jared rubbed his ear, then asked, "We are going dancing, yes?"

The door buzzed.

"Yes." Angelina tugged on his arm as she stepped towards the door. "Come on, let's go in."

Jared pulled the door open and stepped back to let her go in first. The fast paced music of several guitars spilled out into the cool night air.

Stepping into a small foyer, they followed the music up a flight of stairs into a brightly lit ballroom with a dozen-plus people sitting at tables placed around a low wooded stage. Two men sat next to the stage playing guitars as a woman sang in a staccato style unfamiliar to Jared.

Walking among the tables, Angelina chose one close to the stage. Jared pulled out a chair for her and asked, "Where's the dance floor?"

Angelina pointed at the small stage. "There," she said as the two ladies he had met outside stepped up onto it.

The ladies poised, standing back-to-back with one arm raised above their head, while their other hand grasped their dress. The lead guitarist nodded to the women and strummed his guitar to the 12-beat rhythm of an Andalusian song. The spectators at the tables joined in clapping in harmony to the dancer's rhythmic stomping feet.

Having never seen this style of dancing before, Jared stood next to Angelina's chair for the entire song, transfixed with the emotional intensity of the dancers' performance. When the music stopped, he pulled up a chair next to her and whispered, "Will you be up there dancing?"

She wagged her finger. "We will."

Jumping back in his chair, he stammered, "Wh...whoa...whoa."

"Yes, I am." She chuckled. "And, no, I won't make you."

Jared inhaled the scent of her unique perfume as he leaned close to her and gazed into her dark brown eyes before bowing his head. "My humble apologies, you win. You have set this arrogant American straight." Sitting up, he asked, "What's it called?"

"Flamenco." She put her hand on his. "Would you like to learn?"

"If we had something to drink," Jared assured her as he looked around for a waiter, "you would have my full attention."

Angelina rose to her feet. Snapping her fingers above her head while she took toe-heel steps, she walked to a table on the side of the room. Filling two large glasses with wine from a ceramic jug she carried them above her head as she danced back to the table. Placing one in front of Jared, Angelina leaned over and whispered in his ear, "It's self-service."

Jared smiled at hearing her words.

Angelina stood next to him sipping her wine while they watched another dancer on the stage click her heels and whip her dress back and forth to the rhythm of the guitars. When the music stopped, she set her glass on the table and started to rub the side of Jared's head with the tips of her fingers.

Jared raised his hand to entwine his fingers with hers as she whispered, "Four...five...six."

She pulled her hand away at his touch. "My turn to dance next."

Briskly, she walked between the tables, stepped upon the stage and whipped around, turning to face Jared. She grasped her skirt with both hands, arched her right foot onto its toes, and then bowed her head, staring at the floor.

The music started hard and fast.

Angelina raised her head and stared at Jared as she deftly whipped her skirt back and forth. Then forcefully stomping her heels on the wooden floor of the stage to the rhythm, she began to turn to her left, then her right, all the while keeping her eyes focused on him. As the song progressed, she let go of her dress and began to fluidly curve her arms around her body and then over her head as she kept the rhythm with her heels.

As quickly as the music started, it stopped. Angelina then stepped from the platform and walked over to one of the guitar players. She placed her arm around his neck and spoke into his ear. The player shook his head. She patted his cheek, then walked back over to Jared.

"You like it, yes?" she asked and picked up her drink. "I mean my dance."

"Yes." Jared stood up and pulled out her chair for her. "I've never seen anything like it before." After he slid her chair in, he scooted his closer to hers. "My grandfather used to talk about dancing something like this as a child back in the old country."

"Was he a gypsy like me?"

"Not that I know of." Jared looked at his hands as he thought. "He was...from someplace called...Basque. It's near Spain, I think." He took a drink of his wine, adding, "Haven't really got a clue. He passed while I was young."

She shrugged. "He might be, yes?"

Jared, his mind blank as he looked in her eyes, didn't answer.

She stuck her tongue out at him.

"Could you teach me?"

Laughing, she reached over and grabbed his hand, shaking it. "I thought you were going to teach me."

"Give me a few minutes to learn the basics, and then this here master will take over the stage." He drummed his fingers on the table and snickered, "After all, how hard is it to learn to stomp and clap in rhythm?"

"Ok, smart-ass." She sat back in her chair and pointed a finger at him. "Let's see you do the next number."

Jared rose to his feet and undid the buttons on the cuff of his sleeves. "Look out," he grinned while waving his arms, "an American's gonna show you how to do things right." He began to rotate his shoulders in circles and wiggle his arms.

She laughed. "You plan on flying somewhere?"

"Just for that," he pointed a finger at her. "I'm going to show you how easy this boy can win any challenge."

Jared stood next to her, put his hands on his hips. Slightly twisting his back, he stared at her over his shoulder. She snickered and covered her eyes. With the first notes from the guitar, he tapped the side of his leg to get the rhythm, then quickly switched to snapping his fingers. Not moving his feet, he twisted his head one way, then another, while fluttering his eyes at her.

At the end of the song, Jared rubbed his hands together. "Not bad, eh?"

"Oy. You were fantastic." Giggling, Angelina rose to her feet and held out her hand. "It's my turn again. Would you like to come up with me?"

"Ahh, you'll need to excuse me, your highness." Jared kissed the back of her hand. "I need a little more practice. Besides," picking his glass up and holding it at eye level, he pointed to it, "I'm empty."

Angelina silently went over and positioned herself on the stage. From there, she watched Jared pour himself another glass of wine, then quickly down it in one swallow. As he filled the cup again, she looked away and bowed her head.

One of the women Jared had met outside, sauntered over next to him. Pressing her breasts against his arm, she reached around him for an empty cup.

Jared didn't move. Although the pressure on his arm and the aroma of her perfume quickly diverted his attention, he kept his eyes on Angelina's performance.

The woman kept her breasts against his arm as she purred in his ear, "Hmm, so you decided to come in after all. Are you by yourself?"

"No, I'm here with Angelina." Ignoring her overture, he nodded toward the stage. "I should be watching her dance."

She cupped her hand under his chin and gently turned his head. Looking in his eyes, she pursed her lips. "Anytime you want to come over, let me know."

"I really must..." Jared grinned. "But, I'll remember that."

Walking away, he slipped into his chair and clapped enthusiastically for Angelina's performance when the music stopped. She threw him a glance as she stepped off the platform.

Jared hoisted his cup in a gesture of salute to her.

Ignoring him, Angelina stepped over to the guitar players and spoke with the same musician again. The guitarist nodded. She ruffled his hair and walked behind a long row of screens dividing the room.

Jared leaned back and lit a cigarette. Out of a habit picked up in Afghanistan, he started to scan the room and study its occupants. The men, all wore hard-heeled boots, tight pants and button-up shirts. While the women had on long, brightly colored dresses. All were modest in nature, except for Marta and her companion, Sarina. By comparison, theirs were overly tight and quite revealing.

Sarina saw him staring at her. She blew him another kiss and smiled.

Turning to avoid her gaze, he bumped into Angelina's arm. "Oh, sorry."

Angelina reached for her wine. "I see you've met Sarina."

"Is that her name? Yeah, I met her and another lady outside before you came." Jared snorted and shook his head. "They are quite a pair."

"Marta!" Angelina snarled over the rim of her glass. "Be careful of those two sisters."

"What should I have to worry about? They're just two mature women wanting attention."

Pressing the cup of wine to her lips, Angelina glared at Sarina, ignoring his comment.

Jared snubbed out his cigarette, sat back and looked up at her. "And?"

Angelina set her cup down on the table and slid into her chair. "Their family leads our clan."

"So."

"They're wealthy." She folded her arms across her chest. "And dangerous."

Laughing at the look on her face, Jared reached over and tapped the table beside her with his palm. "Can't be anymore dangerous than a guitar player."

"Not funny. He's my brother and those two are trouble." She closed her eyes as he massaged the back of her neck.

"Relax...I'm here with you."

With her eyes still closed, she waved her finger in her brother's direction. "By the way, I...umm." She peeked at Jared. "I asked him to come over to meet you."

He patted her shoulder and rose to his feet. Picking up their empty cups, Jared leaned down and whispered, "He's over at the refreshment table, I'll remind him of what you asked."

Jared walked up behind her brother and placed a hand on his shoulder.

Twisting in agony, Angelina's brother buckled to his knees. Jared grabbed his arm and helped him up. "Hey man, I'm sorry. I didn't know..."

Slowly straightening up, the man snapped, "No problem comrade. You can buy me another cup of coffee tomorrow."

"Hans!" Jared grasped the guy's hand. "Wow. Sorry, I had no idea it was you."

"No worry, I'm OK."

"You really her brother?"

Hans shrugged, "Who?"

"Angelina."

"She is my sister, yes." Grimacing, he hooked his arm around Jared's neck and tugged. "Come, let's go see her."

Hans dropped into the chair across from his sister. "Angelina, why you not tell me you knew my comrade Jared?"

Puzzled, she squinted at Jared. "You know Hans?"

Jared holding the two empty cups in his hands, gave her a toothy grin.

Angelina tugged on Hans sleeve as she growled at him, "Did you put him up to this?"

"Nope." Jared wagged his head and plopped into his chair. "I literally ran into him this morning." Leaning back, he muffled a cough. "Because of our meeting. I got to see more of Amsterdam than I had planned."

Angelina let go of Hans's sleeve and glared at Jared. "You met him on his boat?"

"No." Hans raised his cup and took a sip. "He pulled me off bike this morning. Gave me the bruise on my back."

"You think those two ladies are dangerous." Jared winked at Angelina. "Watch out for me."

"Ah, yes." Hans chuckled. "He has mean right hook."

"Humph." Angelina leaned into Hans's face. "Look what Marta did to you. I'm not laughing."

Hans turned his head away. "You are right." He sat for a moment in silence. Then grinning, he asked Jared, "How would you like to come ride the boat tomorrow?"

"Uh..." Jared sat there rubbing his cheek with his fingers. "I... really should look for work. Being as I couldn't focus on the effort today."

Hans stood up and waved a hand toward the stage. "Great, I see you tomorrow. But I have to play now."

As he walked off, Angelina got up. Grabbing her mantilla, she looked at Jared. "Let's go before all the cabs are taken."

He nodded, and silently followed her out.

Chapter 8

Jared woke up the next morning drenched in sweat. The scar on his chest, throbbed like the day he was wounded in Afghanistan. Swinging his feet to the floor, he sat on the edge of the bed and tapped his cell phone. It was almost ten in the morning.

"Crap," he snarled as he jumped up and jerked his pants on. Ripping a T-shirt from its hanger in the closet, he hopped out the door in an effort to get his shoes on and down the stairs to the dining room before it closed.

His arrival as he burst through the doorless entrance into the breakfast room drew the attention of the landlord sitting in the empty room reading a newspaper.

"Ahh, my friend. Come sit down, I will bring you some coffee."

Jared walked over to the food trays in the steamtable. "You still open? Any eggs left?" Without waiting for an answer, he lifted the covers.

"You may have what is left," the owner answered while he filled a carafe from the large coffee urn. Closing his eyes as he inhaled a whiff of the rising steam from the coffee, the owner asked, "Cream and sugar, yes?"

"Yes, thank you," Jared replied. "How are you doing this morning?"

"I am fine." The owner slid a cup of coffee across the table to Jared. "We missed you at supper. I know it's none of my business, but did you find a job?" Leaning back, the landlord winked. "Or a friend?"

"You're right. It is none of your business." Jared shoveled some eggs into his mouth. "But I will say this, she was a beautiful gypsy."

"Oooh, my friend. Didn't I warn you about those people?" The landlord took a sip of his coffee and smiled. "Did she steal your heart, and then your money?"

"No, actually she stole my heart, then took me to a private dance club." Jared grabbed his coffee, raised it in a salute, then quipped, "and she also paid for the cab fare home."

The landlord sat rigid in his chair with a tense look. "Careful. Those people are up to no good. If you get caught in their camp during a raid, you will be exported." Rubbing his bicep, he added, "I would hate to have you exported, my friend."

"Deported."

"What?"

"It's deported," Jared shot back as he scraped the last bite into his mouth. "And I don't think you'll have to worry about that." He leaned back in his chair and nursed his coffee. "I take it you don't like gypsies?"

The landlord looked at the contents of his cup as he swirled it around. "It's the nature of their culture to steal what they can."

Jared took out a cigarette. "That's not fair to... ." He studied the landlord's face as he lit his lighter. Then it dawned on him. "I see it now. How long ago was it?"

The landlord set his cup down and pressed both hands on the table. After a long pause as he smoothed the table cloth. "I couldn't have been much younger than you. We both worked in the flower fields." Sucking in a breath between his teeth, he smiled. "Ahh, she could sing. As we weeded the fields, she would sing like an angel."

"What happened?" Jared asked, flicking ashes on his plate.

The proprietor stared intently into his cup as if he expected to see her reflection in his coffee. "She played me like a guitar. She knew we could never be together. Her family did not approve of me because I was not a Roma like them. Years ago my family had chosen to give up the itinerant ways and settled down."

"So why didn't you try to convince her to stay?"

"I did. But they moved in the middle of the night."

"And?"

"I followed her to Belgium." He drummed on the table with his fingers. "It was there, her brothers caught us while I was trying to convince her to run away with me." Downing the rest of his coffee, he gritted his teeth. "They beat me and took my money. Then flattened the tires on my car."

Jared wiped his mouth and tossed the napkin on his plate. "Sorry to hear that." Looking at the proprietor, he leaned on the table and asked, "By the way, what's your name? I've been here a week and don't know what to call you."

"Shawn," the landlord answered as he gathered the dishes.

"Sorry, I didn't mean to drag up skeletons from the past."

"No problem, my friend. It's a sunny day and I must get back to work."

Jared rose to his feet. "Yeah, I need to find some work, too." Picking up his cigarettes from the table, he grinned as he asked, "Any particular house of ladies that you might recommend that would be hiring?"

"No, but if you go smelling nice," Shawn lifted the dishes and pointed his nose toward his armpit, "they'll think more kindly of you."

"Oh, yeah. Hey thanks for the advice. I'll catch you later, Shawn."

On his way up the stairs, Jared thought about Shawn's comments about gypsies. In the shower he kept assuring himself Angelina was not that way. As he got dressed, Jared continually glanced out the window of his room. Each time he caught a glimpse of Angelina working across the canal, he stopped to watch her. Then the faint sound of a church bell ringing reminded him of the time.

Picking up the bottle of aftershave on the desk, he slapped some on. "Not exactly the greatest, but it couldn't hurt."

When he stepped out onto the street, he stayed on his side of the canal so as not to be tempted to stop and visit with Angelina. Instead, he walked the several blocks up to the next bridge and crossed over the water before weaving his way through the narrow streets and passageways into the Red Light district.

A little nervous as he came to the first house, he snubbed out his cigarette and tossed it into a trash can. With his hand still on the lid, he took a deep breath. "They speak English, just relax." Then exhaling a second breath, his face went flush. "Whoa, asking a prostitute for work...just ain't right." He let go of the lid, turned toward the door and smoothed his shirt. "Relax. This ain't the first time you been around these kind of girls," he muttered to himself.

Knocking on the door, he smoothed his shirt once more and stepped back. A slender dark-haired woman in her late twenties answered the door, "Ja?"

"I was wondering if I could have a job."

She tapped the small sign in the door's window. "Come back when I'm open."

"I mean, do you need someone—"

She slammed the door shut before he could finish.

By the time the fourth door slammed shut in his face, he began to relax in his approach to the ladies. But, he still had to convince himself at each door he wasn't seeking to work in the sex industry.

At the sixth door he knocked on, a woman in her forties slid open the glass door. Leaning against the doorjamb, she looked at Jared with a blank stare while he asked his question. After he finished, she smiled, "You're new to the game, aren't you?"

"Yes ma'am. But I'm a fast learner."

"Not fast enough." She pulled her silk robe across her chest, then folded her arms. "I just hired someone an hour ago. Too bad. I would have hired you."

Jared raised his eyebrows. "How about tomorrow?"

She took a cigarette from her robe pocket and lit it. "Sorry honey, out of cards. But I got time for a show if you want."

Jared coughed as he tried to stifle his laughter. "I'm sure I would enjoy it, but I need a job. Not to mention my girlfriend would be upset."

The prostitute winked. "I won't tell."

"No thanks."

She pulled a card from her pocket and held it out to him. "If you change your mind."

"Touché." Jared took the card.

For the next hour he continued to knock on doors, unwilling to give up even though he was frustrated with having so many close in his face. Then as he walked along the second-to-the-last block, he passed a glass door to what appeared to be an empty space for rent. A sudden movement in the corner stopped him. Jared backed up and tapped on the glass. The figure rose up from behind a large overstuffed chair with a broom in her hands and answered, "Yes?"

Jared stood there speechless as he looked at the tall blonde wearing only a tiny crocheted bra and a thong.

"Come back tonight when I'm open."

Jared blinked. "Sorry. I'm...a...do you have any advertisement cards you want handed out?"

She slid the door open. "You don't look the type. But if you come back tomorrow, I'll give you ten euros for every two hundred fifty you pass out."

Thrusting out his hand, Jared smiled. "What time?"

She glanced at his hand. "Ten in the morning." Sliding the door closed, she went back to work.

Jared waited until her back was turned and then pumped his fist. "Yes!"

Seeing there was no one in the last booth, he decided to call it a day and find out where Hans docked his boat. Maybe he would take that boat ride after all.

Chapter 9

Searching for the address of Hans's tour boat with his cell phone, Jared found that it was about ten blocks away and two canals over. Careful to read the street signs as he weaved his way through the central part of the city, he found the docking location just as Hans's boat pulled alongside.

After the last passenger left, Hans tied a rope across the ramp and pointed down the street. "Break time. Let's go for coffee."

Looking at the boat as he walked away, Jared asked, "What kind of tours do you do?"

"Mostly make big circles."

"Huh?"

"I go down this canal to red light house and stop. People get off, people get on. Then go to museum for pictures and stop." Hans reached for the cafe door. "Then stop at Jewish girl's house, who die in war. Then go to next museum before entering other canal."

Jared followed him inside to a table by the window. "What kind of touristy thing is that, where they can get on and off like it was a city bus?"

"Exactly." Hans nodded at a waiter and held up two fingers. "Same as bus, but boat. How you do finding job?"

Lighting a cigarette, Jared nodded. "Great. I got one lady who said to come back tomorrow for ten Euros."

Hans whistled. "Do you get big discount from the seventy-five for show?"

Jared snorted, "I wish." He rubbed his face with his palm. "Ten Euros, for what I guess to be about two hours' work. Even if I did it eight hours a day, it wouldn't pay the rent."

"Will take you three hours to pass them out on good day." Hans nodded as he held up three fingers. "Unless you throw them in the trash and take the money."

'I can't do that, it's stealing." Jared took a puff from his cigarette as their coffee was set before them. "There's got to be something I can do that doesn't...."

Hans ripped open a packet of sugar and poured it in his coffee. "I feel for you, man. I went through same thing when sister and me came here first time."

"What? I thought I heard Sarina was your aunt?"

"She not really aunt. Her son is king of local gypsy clan. So in way we are related."

Jared picked up a packet of sugar and shook it. "So what's that got to do with the world?" Tearing it open, he poured it in his coffee. "I mean, I know nothing about gypsies, other than the fact no one likes them."

Hans choked on his coffee. "That's what make it so hard to get job." He wiped his mouth. "I couldn't get job like you. Then Angelina met Sarina. She gave her job at cafe to keep her safe."

"Safe from what?"

Flicking a few grains of sugar off the table, Hans shrugged, "Gypsy culture has strict customs."

Jared dropped his cigarette into the ashtray, then reached for another packet of sugar. "You've got me lost. What does...I mean they didn't teach us about gypsies in school." He scratched the underside of his jaw before tearing open the paper packet. "So how did all this get you a job?"

Hans picked up Jared's pack of cigarettes from the table and shook a half-dozen of them into his hand. "OK." Laying them down in a circle like they were the spokes of a wheel, and with his finger circling the outer edge of the cigarettes, he started to explain. "All gypsies work together for good of group." He pointed at the center. "They pay tribute to king of local clan. If king likes you, he helps you find job." Hans picked up one of the cigarettes rolling it between his fingers. "If not...you are like smoke."

Jared set his cup down and snatched a cigarette from the circle. "I think you been smokin' too much of that other stuff, my friend. 'Cause I still don't know what you're talking about."

Hans dropped the cigarette and leaned back . "Marta's son owns car rental business and Sarina's family owns several canal boats along with cafe. If you talk to them, you might get job."

Jared picked up the pack and put the cigarettes back in. "Are you kidding? Angelina has already expressed her dislike for those two."

"You want job? Or cower to her demands?"

Jared shoved the pack into his shirt pocket with a grin. "I'm not gonna play that game. Your sister means too much to me."

"No problem," Hans mused. "I've heard you Americans are—"

"Now wait a minute," Jared tapped the table. "You ain't pullin' that one either."

"What? That you American men cower to woman's demands?"

Rubbing the top of his head, Jared winced at the comment. "OK, OK, let me think about."

Hans swirled his coffee. "Car rental need people all the time to move cars around."

"Look," Jared jabbed his finger at Hans, "I'm not a gypsy and you said that's important. What makes you think I have a chance with them?"

"They are from Kalderash clan. Me and Angelina are Sevitka Roma." Hans set his cup down. "I give you another lesson. Sevitka are smarter than Kalderash, we stay in school longer."

Jared rolled his eyes and emptied his cup.

Hans held up his finger. "One moment. You told Angelina your grandfather from Basque homeland. Yes?"

He cocked his head and stared at Hans. "So?"

"Many gypsies live in same homeland. You are Gadjo."

"I thought you said you were Sevitka?"

Hans wagged his finger at Jared. "Ahh. You have no Romanipen. That's how we get you job."

"What are you talking about?"

Hans sat there rubbing his head. "You truly have no Romanipen." Leaning on his elbow, he gently scratched his eyebrow. "Our mother only gypsy, our father is Ukraine. Because our father raised us alone after our mother die, we also Gadjo." He looked out the window while waving two fingers. "Uhmm, two class gypsy."

"You mean second class?"

"Mmm, yes." Hans drummed his fingers on the table. "No. We neither wanted, nor shunned. Just used for their benefit."

Jared snorted. "Isn't that what I said?"

"No, different." Hans glanced at his watch. "Maybe I go with you and talk for you."

"Absolutely not. If Angelina heard either one of us went to Sarina's house," Jared rolled his eyes, "I'd never hear the end of it."

"Ha ha, you don't know how."

"The hotel owner where I stay says gypsy women can't have a relationship with a non-gypsy man." Jared knocked on the table. "And I don't wan—"

"He's right." Hans got up out of his chair. "Break over. Come ride, we'll talk more."

Jared stood and started for the door. Hans stepped beside him. "Don't worry my friend." He put his arm around Jared's shoulder. "That is old custom. It is dying out. My sister likes you and I like you. But you need to learn how to handle gypsy women."

"Hah!" Jared stepped away from Hans and squinted at him with one eye. "Oh really? How come you're afraid of Marta and Sarina?"

Hans fingered the employee badge clipped to his shirt. "They are different."

"I'll say they are. The night I met them..." Jared whistled.

Walking in front of the small group of tourists waiting to board his boat, Hans began collecting tickets as he loudly declared, "Careful of step please." Helping an older woman onto the ramp, he glanced over at Jared. "Careful brother, those two are dangerous."

Jared followed Hans on board. "I thought you said women—"

Hans turned the key in the ignition switch and revved the motor. "Must I teach you everything?"

"Yes, sahib." Jared laughed and touched his forehead, then twirled his hand. "I await your words of wisdom."

Hans took hold of the microphone hanging next to the steering wheel. "Good afternoon, ladies and gentlemen, please stay seated while boat is in motion." He put the mic down by his side and leaned over to Jared. "Angelina works late tonight. Meet me at her cafe. Maybe...five? I give you first lesson."

Pulling a cigarette out of his pocket, Jared lit it and exhaled. "OK, but I don't—"

The woman sitting in front of Jared turned around and snatched the cigarette out of his mouth. "No smoking!" she snapped and flicked it into the canal.

"What?" He looked at the woman, then over at Hans.

Hans grinned as he nodded and pointed to the sign in five different languages on the side of the boat. "That lesson one."

"Wow," Jared rubbed his hands together, "and to think, I thought re-adjusting to life would be easier here."

"It is OK. Kick back and enjoy, my friend." Hans keyed the microphone again. "This canal was build in..."

Chapter 10

While passing out advertisement cards the next day for the "red light lady", Jared scored more work from several of the other prostitutes to fill out the day.

Carefully, he timed his approach to the crowds of tourists outside the trinket shops, hoping it would lead to one of the shops hiring him, or at least help him pass out cards faster. He didn't care what kind of a job he did, as long as it paid more. His enthusiasm got him several offers from the souvenir shops, but each was retracted when he couldn't produce the necessary work documents.

After the end of his first day handing out cards, Jared went over to Angelina and Hans's flat, and spent the evening on a bench outside their apartment building with them. Hans played his guitar, while Angelina tried to teach Jared the basic steps to flamenco dancing.

Unable to master the footwork, he often stumbled and fell into Angelina's arms. Laughing, she would gaze into his eyes and flutter her lashes. Jared, on cue, would make a joke about the "new" style he was teaching her.

Hans rolled his eyes after the umpteenth time of hearing that line, stopped and asked, "Jared, you found work yet? I know somebody who hire you."

Angelina choked at hearing her brother's words and turned away from Jared. She folded her arms, glaring at her brother first, then at Jared.

Jared sighed and dropped onto the bench next to Hans. "Not really, not yet."

Angelina shook her head and went inside the building.

"Thanks a lot, Hans. I almost..." Jared exhaled loudly as he pulled out a cigarette. "She's..." he waved it in the air, "she's—"

"My sister," Hans interrupted. Resting his guitar on his foot, he looked down the street at some children playing and added, "As oldest man in family, it's my job."

"Sorry, man. I understand, I have a little sister too." Leaning forward, his elbows on his knees, Jared looked up at the building. "Everybody keeps asking for work documents. Where do you get 'em?"

"You have to get work first. Employer get for you."

TWO EVENINGS LATER, while they were hanging around the bench dancing again, Jared fell into Angelina's arms and she nuzzled his neck while cooing in his ear. Hans stopped playing and took a drink of his beer. Swallowing, he asked, "Jared, you find work today?"

Not wanting to screw it up this time, Jared blurted out, "I would rather find work on my own. I don't want to be beholden to the sisters for my job."

Smiling, Angelina gave him a hug. "Thank you. It means a lot to me." She sat on the bench and patted it next to her. "I think you might make a good dancer yet."

Sitting beside her, Jared reached behind her shoulders and touched Hans.

Hans glanced over at him.

Jared looked into Angelina's eyes as he gave Hans a thumbs-up. "You really think so? I mean I came here to teach you how to dance."

Hans shook his head.

She jabbed him in the ribs. "You don't have any rhythm, let alone able to carry a tune."

Jared leaned in front of Angelina. "Hans, let me borrow your guitar."

Hans held it out slowly. "Don't break guitar like some crazy rock star."

"Humm," Jared weighted the instrument with his hands, "nice. Do you have a pick?"

"A what?"

"Never mind, I'll try it without one." Jared strummed the stings a few times before playing "Mary Had a Little Lamb."

Angelina covered her mouth and laughed. "OK, I was wrong."

Jared grinned and started the next verse before quickly shifting from the children's rhyme to a hard rock blues song.

Dumbfounded, she listened to him play while Hans bobbed his head and tapped his thigh to the rhythm of the song.

With the last few notes of the ten-minute song, Jared closed his eyes, smiling to himself. Satisfied, he opened them and continued to smile while he strummed the strings once more, then played another electric blues tune. Frantically fingering the frets, he closed his eyes as he played for fifteen minutes.

When the sound of the last cord died, he held the guitar out to Hans. "Thank you. I wasn't sure if I could still do it."

"What?" Hans took hold of his guitar. "That was fantastic. You must teach me that song."

"You were great." Angelina hugged Jared and rubbed his back. "How come you've never played for us before?"

"Because." Jared shrugged and slid his hand through his short hair. " I swore I'd never play again after my roommate Kevin was killed from a mortar round. It all happened because I was outside playing so he could sleep."

Angelina leaned her head on his shoulder. "Please, don't blame yourself. You didn't know."

Jared stiffened. "You don't understand. The Taliban zeroed in on the sound of my guitar and hit our hooch."

Angelina touched his cheek, looking him in the eyes. "You don't know that for sure."

He glared at her. "They hated our music. They said it was —"

She put her finger over his lips. "Let it go. You're here now."

Jared pulled away and stood up. "That's easy for you to say, you weren't there."

Hans, cradling his guitar, tried to copy a few cords from the first song Jared played. "I don't quite remember how the song went." Holding out the instrument, he asked, "Would you play once more for me?"

Jared looked at the ground. Biting his lip, he sighed.

Angelina touched his hand. "Please. I'd like to hear it again too."

He took a deep breath and exhaled. "Yeah, why not."

Chapter 11

After playing many of the songs he knew for Hans and Angelina, Jared took a cab back to his hotel. As he stepped from the cab, a helicopter flew overhead. Looking up, he watched the aircraft's lights move across the sky. Suddenly a loud boom echoed in the distance. Jared dropped to his knees beside the cab searching for where the explosion came from.

The cab driver yelled out the open door, "You OK?"

Jared blinked, and silently nodded as he rose to his feet. Closing the car door he walked across the sidewalk toward the hotel. The aircraft circled around and hovered overhead. He looked up at it just as another loud boom echoed in the distance.

He dove into a basement stairwell for cover. Slowly peeking over the sidewalk, he expected a firefight to erupt any second. A third boom echoed, this time with a metallic rattle. Jared dropped down in the stairwell cursing, "Where the hell are they? Lonnie...John...can anybody see their position?"

Another boom echoed, followed by the double toot from a train horn.

With his back against the concrete wall, Jared sucked in a deep breath and cradled his head at the realization of what the noise really was. He lit a cigarette and sat listening to the sounds drifting through the cool night air from the freight yard. After a few puffs, he climbed out of the stairwell and briskly walked around the corner to the hotel's entrance. Inside, he ran up the stairs to his room and grabbed the bottle of bourbon off the dresser. With trembling, sweaty hands, he fought to get the cap off. Unable to get a good grip, Jared put it in his mouth and bit down on the cap, then twisted it off. Spitting the cap on the desk, he tilted the bottle back and poured the golden-brown liquor down his throat. A quarter of the bottle's contents disappeared before he gasped for breath and slammed the bottle down on the dresser. Wiping his face with his sleeve, he dove onto his bed and buried his face in the pillow.

He woke up at two a.m. and the sheets were soaked with sweat. Crawling off the bed, he pulled a cigarette from its pack on the desk, then settled into the overstuffed easy chair next to it. In the dim moonlight entering through the window, he leaned over and grabbed the bourbon off the dresser. Jared stared at the opposite wall for what seemed like forever, then took a hefty swig. Trading the bottle for his lighter lying on the desk, he lit the cigarette, and then rubbed his eyes and forehead as his thoughts ran together. Exasperated, he tossed the lighter on the desk and snatched up the bottle resting it on his leg. Raising the bottle to take a drink he saw the TV remote. Instead he picked it up and turned the television on.

Surfing through the channels, Jared came across a music video of Golden Earring playing "Twilight Zone." The song was his favorite during his deployment. He turned the sound up. The pounding of his heart quickly matched the rhythm of the bass drum. As he lifted the bottle taking a drink, the song came to the line, *when the bullet hits the bone*, he shuddered and remembered he was answering Dave's question about the words when the RPG hit. Jared bit his lip and took a deep breath. Then the TV spit out the line, *all circuits are dead,* he nodded in agreement and hefted the bottle taking another swig. Slowly, Jared set the clicker on the arm of the chair and nimbly felt the bullet scar on his chest.

Suddenly a gunshot from the song filled his ears and echoed in the room. The television instantly became a blur and his surroundings faded to grey, while Afghanistan filled his conscious being. The chair he was sitting in, became hard as rock and as large as a boulder. The smoke from his cigarette smelled of gunpowder. Looking down, Dave lay on the floor, staring at him. Jared pushed back against the rock and screeched, "Why? Why did it have to be you?"

A loud commercial on the television broke in screaming, "Hey you! Hey you!"

Jared shook his head and Dave disappeared.

With Dave gone, Jared felt the pain of the cigarette burning his fingers. Shaking the butt from his hand, he licked his burn and looked around for the bottle that had been in his other hand. A trail of liquor led under the bed.

Jared slid out of the chair and retrieved the bottle. Holding it up, the flickering light from the television danced inside the clear glass bottle, playing with his eyes. Drinking what was left, he walked over to the window. Staring through the trees along the canal, he looked down at the empty cafe. The thought of Angelina's smile soothed his headache enough to turn off the television and crawl back into bed.

But the demons still tormented him the rest of the night.

JARED WOKE UP AT NOON and groaned as he tried to sit up. His head throbbed. He glanced around in search of the time. Finally, the red digits on the clock across the room came into focus. He exhaled a loud airy curse as he rose and stumbled to the window. It was raining, and no one was sitting outside at the cafe. Coughing, he turned, picked up his shaving kit and a towel, then headed for the shared bathroom down the hall.

Back in his room, Jared opened the window. Leaning out, he looked up and down the canal at the empty sidewalks. "No tourists, no work, no money. Crap."

He snuffed out his cigarette in the ashtray on the window ledge and turned back into the room. "Gonna need to find something else for work. Maybe Shawn's got an idea."

With the empty liquor bottle in hand, he went downstairs to the breakfast room. He could hear Shawn humming as he worked in the kitchen. Jared dropped the empty bottle in the garbage can, then poured himself a cup of coffee. Carefully holding the cup with two hands, he went over and sat at the table closest to the kitchen door. Inhaling the coffee's aroma made it easier to breathe, while at the same time reminded him of one of his nightmares. Shivering at the thought, he spilled some of the hot liquid on his hand. "Damn!" Jared dropped the cup.

Shawn peeked around the corner. "Ahh, my friend, be careful." He ducked back into the kitchen. Stepping out, he threw Jared a towel. "Here."

Jared caught the cloth. "Thanks."

"You are up late." Shawn hollered from the kitchen. "I've put everything away."

"That's OK, I don't feel like eating anyway," Jared said as he got up and refilled his cup.

The kitchen went quiet. Shawn appeared around the corner, wiping his hands on a towel. He walked over to the coffee pot and poured himself a cup. He saw the empty bottle in the garbage can. "Rough night, yes?"

Jared blew on his coffee. "You might say that."

Shawn slipped into the chair across the table. "Your gypsy friend?"

Jared shook his head. "Her, I can handle." Slurping at the hot liquid he moaned, "I need something to do ... something to occupy my mind."

"Like work?"

"Yes."

"I thought you were passing out cards for the ladies."

Jared set his cup down. "That's not enough, I need something to give my life meaning."

"Ahh, the man thing." Shawn leaned back. "Work gives his life meaning." He brushed at a crumb on the table. "Women take that into consideration, too. No work, no women."

"No. No, Angelina's not like that. It's just that I..." Pressing his knuckles against his lips, Jared looked out the window. "It's just like I said. I need a job."

"Didn't you say you knew the gypsy king's mother?" Shawn pulled a package of crackers from his apron, leaning forward, he slid them to Jared. "Ask her to have a talk with her son."

Rolling his eyes, Jared chortled, "Angelina would kill me."

"Are you a man or a mouse?"

"It's not that simple."

"Why not? You were a soldier, yes?"

"That's the point." Jared gripped his cup tighter. "She gives me a reason."

Shawn stared at his hand as he rubbed his thumb around his palm. "Ahh, he paid you a visit last night."

"No." Jared blinked at Shawn. "I was... who?"

"Your shadow."

Jared sat back. "What are you talking about?"

Shawn, wiping at a drop of coffee on the table, queried, "A friend from the war visited last night, yes?"

"No one was in my room but me."

"OK," the proprietor picked up his cup, "if you say so."

Jared swallowed the last of his coffee, rubbed the back of his teeth with his tongue and stared at Shawn.

The proprietor stood up. "If I were in your feet, I would pay that gypsy woman a visit. You might get lucky and find work."

Jared grinned. "Shoes."

"What?"

Jared stood up. "It's, if I were in your shoes."

"OK." Shawn took Jared's cup from him and headed for the kitchen. "Have a good day, my friend."

Chapter 12

Jared ran down the street to where Hans tied his boat up. After copying the company's information from the sign into his phone, he quickly hailed a taxi to take him to their office on the edge of the city.

The address was a low-slung business complex surrounded by a vast expanse of fields on three sides. "Oh great," Jared groaned as he climbed out of the cab. "This is going to be fun going door to door trying to match names."

Finished with the first row of buildings, he walked toward the second row and saw three Mercedes with tinted windows parked at the far end of the complex. He briefly looked around the empty parking lot. "Why do I get the feeling that that's the place?"

He walked past the first three offices with a hurried look at their door, then stopped in front of the first Mercedes. "Sweet willy. I'd give my eye teeth for one of those." He held his phone up to compare the name on the office door. "Yep, this is the place."

Jared pulled on the door handle; it was locked. He pressed his face against the glass in the door and could see someone at a desk in an inner office. "Well... here it goes." He pushed the buzzer.

"Ja?"

"Uhmm, I'm here looking for a job."

The reply came back in Dutch, from which he was able to pick out the words "no" and "work."

Desperate, he pushed the buzzer again.

"Ja?"

"Hello, my name is Jared. I'm here looking for Sarina."

"She is not here."

"Oh!" Jared bit his lip and stepped away from the door.

The door lock clicked.

He waited, hesitant to reach for it.

It swung open. Marta held the door ajar with her foot. "Why do you want to see her?"

Jared stepped back surprised at seeing Marta. "She, uh, she offered me a job last week at the club and I came by to see if that option was still available."

Marta grinned. "I think that job was for one night only."

Jared blushed at his misunderstanding. "Oh."

"You're Angelina's friend, aren't you?"

He pushed his shoulders back. "Yes."

"Come in." Marta held the door open. "I might have a use for someone like you."

Jared paused; he didn't like how she said that. Gritting his teeth, he stepped inside.

Marta let the door swing close and asked, "Hold out your hands."

He blinked at the question, then promptly did as she asked.

"Can you drive?"

He watched as she turned his hands over, inspecting them. "Yes, I have an American license and an International one, too."

She dropped his hands. "Hmm, good. How much time is left on your passport?"

Jared took a deep breath. "I think about five or six years."

She walked around behind him. "Ever been arrested in the E.U.?"

He moaned at her question. "Yeah, in Frankfurt. For brawling."

The fifty-ish woman put her hand on the back of his shoulder and felt the tone of his muscles. "What do you call *brawling*?"

Jared shivered at the sensation of her hand on his back. "Fighting."

Marta slid her hand along his back as she walked to his other side. "Hmm, did you win?"

"You might say that. I was told it took five Polizei to put the cuffs on me."

He winched as she smacked his butt. "I might have a place for you. Can you control your drinking?"

He turned glaring at her. "I'm not a drunk, if that is what you are insinuating."

Marta grinned. "Uhmm, spunky aren't we. Angelina says your ex-military, is that correct?"

Jared relaxed a little bit. "Two tours in Afghanistan."

She turned and walked toward her office. "Follow me."

"Yes, ma'am."

Marta hesitated at hearing his words. Smiling, she nodded to herself and continued thru the doorway. "Have a seat." She pointed to the empty chair next to her desk and walked around to her chair. "Do you need a map when you're driving, or do you know how to make your phone work for you?"

"I found this place, didn't I?"

Pulling a set of car keys from her desk drawer, she held them in her hand. "I need someone to take this Audi to our lot in Munich. By tomorrow morning."

Jared whistled. "That's pushing it. I was hoping to take Ange—"

"You want the job?"

Looking at the keys, he asked, "How do I get back?"

"You'll take one of our cars from Munich to our lot in Budapest. They'll have one that needs to come back here."

"And if they don't?"

Marta turned, opened an under-counter refrigerator and took two bottles of water from it. "Don't worry, you'll bring a car back. That's the way the business works." She handed him a bottle. "You just won't return the same route you left on."

Jared twisted the top off. "OK, I think I understand. Product availability for the tourists." He took a drink. "What's it pay?"

Marta sat back. "That depends on you. At each lot you'll be given five hundred euros, and whatever is left over is yours."

Smacking his lips, he whistled. Suddenly, the grin left his face. "Wait a minute. I have to pay for the gas?"

Drumming her long fingernails on the desk, Marta reiterated, "Whatever it costs. Petrol, food, tolls, tickets, whatever. Stay out of the brothels, too. I won't tolerate tardiness."

Jared leaned across the desk and held out his hand. "You've got yourself a deal."

Marta grabbed his hand, shaking it as she stood. "Good." Letting go, she pulled an envelope from the desk drawer and dropped it next to the keys. "Munich, by tomorrow."

"Whoa, that doesn't leave me any time to go by my room and pay ahead on the rent."

She glanced at her fingernails, then at him. "Did I forget to mention you'll be moving to my villa and cleaning the pool while you're not on the road?"

Jared set the keys and envelope down. "Tempting. But Angelina won't go for it."

Marta gave him a wicked smile. "Who does she work for?"

Taking a deep breath, he bit his lip and squinted at the keys. Snatching them back up, he crooned, "I'll still need to swing by and pay the rent."

"If it's any consolation, I'll send Angelina and Hans over to collect your belongings. They'll bring everything to my place."

"Do I have a choice?"

"No."

Exhaling loudly through pursed lips, he shoved the envelope in his pocket. "Where to in Munich?"

Marta held out a business card. "When you get within fifty kilometers of the city you are delivering to, call this number."

"And if I break down?"

"If you can't fix it yourself, call that number."

Jared looked at the simple black and yellow card. "Anything else?"

She took a sip of water. "Yes. Hold onto all the envelopes your money comes in, till you get back here. And make sure the delivery envelopes are in the glove box before you turn the car over."

"What? You got—"

"Recycling laws."

"I thought that... oh never mind." He stuffed the card in his shirt pocket. "Where's the car?"

Chapter 13

It was a hectic three-days of driving from Amsterdam to Munich to Budapest to Milan, then back to Amsterdam. Arriving at Marta's office early in the morning before anyone else, Jared leaned the driver's seat back and tried going to sleep. But as luxurious as the Fiat Spider was, it was too uncomfortable to nod off in. He put the convertible roof down in the early sunshine and pulled his cap over his eyes. In the warmth of the rays, he was finally able to drift off.

Awaken by a knock on the car's door, Jared mumbled, "What?"

"Inside." Marta's voice was curt.

"Yeah, sure." He opened the door, half falling/half stumbling out of the car. "Not even a hello. Or, great you're back." He stretched the kink out of his back then sauntered over to the office door. It was locked. He pushed the button.

Marta flicked the lights on in her office, then buzzed him in.

Jared stumbled in and tossed the keys onto the desk in front of her. "Here. Is there any coffee around?"

She pointed towards the office door. "Around the corner."

Stepping out into the hallway, he returned with a cup in hand and then flopped into the empty chair next to her desk. "Phfft, that's hot," he sputtered and set the cup on her desk. Sucking in a deep breath, Jared rubbed his face with both hands.

Marta sat back in her chair. "Where's the envelopes you were given?"

Jared snorted. "I thought you said the money was mine."

"I did." She held out her hand. "I want the envelopes you were given."

"Oh." Opening each brown envelope, he took the cash out and tossed the empty envelope on her desk. "I get it, you people are really into recycling." Flipping the last one over, he stared at its blank outside before handing it to her. "But, whatever floats your boat."

Marta's expression didn't change. "Go home and rest."

"I can't. You moved me to your place." He picked up his coffee and took a sip. "Haven't got a clue where that's at."

Marta pushed the intercom button on her office phone. "Cheryl. Call Jared a taxi."

"Yes, ma'am."

"Hand this to the driver," Marta explained while writing an address on a sticky note. "Your room is downstairs. End of the hallway on the left."

Jared peeled the note off her outstretched hand. "How about breakfast?"

"The others already know you are coming and will have everything prepared."

Tired and hungry, Jared sat there staring at the picture on the wall behind her, wondering what he had gotten himself into.

"Jared ... Jared." Marta snapped her fingers.

"Huh?"

"Your taxi is here. Go home and get some rest."

Wiping his face, he stood up. "Yeah, OK."

Coffee in hand, he stumbled out the door to the waiting cab. Opening the car door, Jared stuck his leg in to sit down when the driver snapped, "No drinks."

Swallowing a mouthful of the hot drink, he set the cup on the ground. "Here," Jared sighed and slid onto the plush leather seat, handing the driver Marta's address.

"HOLY SMOKES, WHAT A house." Jared stood at the bottom of the front steps, gawking the Chateau style villa where the taxi dropped him off. At the top of the steps, he looked around at the walled grounds in front of the house as he knocked on the door. "Wow, the perks with this job. I can't believe Angelina's attitude against her aunts."

He knocked again; no answer.

Twisting the doorknob, he found it was locked.

"Now what?" Jared muttered as he stepped away from the large oak door. Studying the architecture of the entrance, he finally noticed the doorbell button and pushed it.

No response.

"Phfft, locked out." He turned around to face the gate. "I wondered about this happening."

Suddenly, from a hidden speaker, a voice boomed, "Ja?"

Jared looked up, searching for where the voice came from. "Hi, I'm Jared. Marta said—"

The door lock buzzed and clicked, allowing the door to swing slightly ajar.

He pushed it open further and looked around the large reception hall. "Hello?" His voice welcomed him as it echoed.

He stepped in and swung the door shut behind him. "OK. Down the stairs, end of hall."

Habitually pulling out a cigarette, he started to light it. "Whoops, better not." He snapped his lighter closed and shoved it in his pocket. Confidently, he placed the cigarette behind his ear and asked himself, "Now where would I hide the stairs down in a place like this?"

An alcove in the corner of the room next to the front door caught his attention. "Ah, that's gotta be... a coat room? I'll bet that's where it's hidden." In the alcove's entrance, he glanced around. "I was right. A coat room, but no stairs."

Turning around and stepping back into the hall, he was surprised by a young boy of about ten years, in the middle of the reception hall. "Oh, hey, my name is Jared. I'm looking for the stairs to my room."

Not flinching, the boy stared at him as he spun a soccer ball between his hands.

"Uh, let's see," Jared uttered. "How do I say that in Dutch?" He snapped his finger. "I got it." Holding up his hand, he used two fingers to mimic walking across a floor. Then as he tried to illustrate going down stairs, he spoke a few words in German, "Nein uber, eine...eine auf."

The boy shook his head. Then with a smirk, he pointed to a narrow doorway behind a statue of David. "If you're looking for the stairs to the servant's quarters, they're through that door." Bouncing the ball on the floor, he walked out the front door.

Jared crooned as he rubbed the back of his neck, "That's what I love about Europe; nobody speaks English, but everybody does. Sheesh, I'm gonna love this job."

Chapter 14

It was three in the afternoon when Jared finally got out of bed and strolled down the hall in search of the bathroom. Finding a small shared washroom for the servants, he leaned over and splashed water on his face from one of the four sinks located back to back in its center. *Looks like the Army all over again,* he thought as he glanced around the room. *Wonder where the commodes are?*

Two louvered half-doors were on the left side of the room, walking over, he opened one. "Ha, there we go." He stepped in and let the door swing shut. "At least the toilet's a quiet modern style and not the old chamber pots."

"I'll bet those are the showers," he quipped as he stepped out of the water closet and looked at the two full-height louvered doors across the room.

Jared washed his hands, then wiped them on his pants as he went over and reached for one of the door handles. Before he could touch it, the door swung out, hitting his hand.

The teenage girl wrapped in a wet towel behind the door let out a startled scream when she saw him.

Jared jumped back. "I'm sorry. I didn't mean to scare you."

Gripping her shampoo bottle tight by her side, she growled, "Who are you?"

"I'm Jared. I work for Marta." He took another step back. "Who might you be?"

The rather tall teenager folded her arms across her chest, eyeing him. "I'm Sarina's daughter, Kris."

"Umm, what are you doing down here in the servant's quarters?" he asked as he leaned to see around her into the shower.

A smirk rolled across her face. "What do you think?" She gripped her towel and started to unwrap it. "Or would you like to see?"

Spinning on his heels, Jared headed for the door. He held it open, then paused with his back toward her. "Who else uses these facilities?"

"Just me, my brother, and Olga the cook. The rest of the family are on the upper floors."

"Your brother..., is he about ten years old?"

"Yes."

"OK," Jared whispered. He looked at his phone. "Hupt, nice meeting you, but I need to get moving if I'm going to make it."

AS HE CLIMBED OUT OF the cab, he looked first at the hotel, then across the canal towards the cafe. "Ahh, think I better go over and see Angelina first before talking to Shawn."

Sitting at a table next to the water, Jared kept an eye out for Angelina as he took a small package from his pocket and placed it on the table. Minutes later she stepped out with an order in her hands. When she spotted him, she paused.

Jared smiled and waved.

Her sour expression didn't change, until she placed the order in front of one of her customers. Then she smiled for them.

Smiling, Jared waited for her.

Angelina ignored him and went back inside.

Thinking nothing of it, Jared picked up the package, opened the small box and looked at the locket.

Angelina came out and silently walked by him on her way to another table. Noticing her, Jared put the gift down and held up his hand. "Hi. I'm—"

She coldly brushed past him.

Rolling his eyes, he took out a cigarette, lighting it.

A few minutes later, with a cup of coffee in one hand and a glass of water in the other, she walked by, and without breaking stride, slid the coffee onto his table. Much of the hot liquid spilled and rolled into his lap.

Jared yelped, "Hello to you, too," as he jumped up, tugging at his wet jeans.

Without looking back, she continued to walk on to another table. With a smile, she gave them their water. Her smile disappeared as she turned and brushed by him, taking an empty bread basket held up by another customer.

Jared pushed the cup away and dabbed at the wet spot on his jeans.

When she finally came out again, Angelina skirted to the far side of the tables, approaching a new customer.

Maybe Shawn was right about her, he thought as she looked through him with cold eyes.

Defiant, Jared rose, snatched the gift off the table. "No, ain't gonna let it happen," he barked. Weaving around the tables, he stepped into Angelina's path. "Angie, I'm sorry. OK?"

She stared him in the eyes as she folded her arms.

"Look," he bit his lip, "I was wrong for not seeing you before I left."

"You didn't even call."

"But I needed the job. And she said go now."

"I found out you were gone when Hans picked me up to pack your things."

"I know." Jared glanced at his feet, then at her. "Things didn't go the way I hoped."

"I warned you about her."

"You said she was dangerous." He grinned. "Besides, she's an older woman wanting attention."

Angelina looked at him thru narrow slits and growled, "That's not what I meant."

Jared put his hand on her arm. "Then what?"

She looked down at the dishes in her hands. "I dunno. There's something about those two. I just can't put my finger on it."

"Hey, I screwed up, OK? I should have called you while I was gone. But...will this show you that I was thinking of you the whole time?" He opened the small box in his hand and pulled out a thin gold chain with a heart-shaped locket hanging from it. "I picked it up in Milan while I was waiting for them to finish with the car."

"That depends." Her eyes lit up as she gently held the locket in her fingers. "Is dinner included?"

Jared undid the clasp. "Anywhere you want."

Angelina turned around. "And dancing?"

He draped the chain around her neck. "Sure."

She turned back around, "Seven?"

Jared started to wrap his arms around her when the cook whistled for Angelina.

She kissed him on the cheek. "Gotta go."

Chapter 15

After a night of clubbing with Angelina, Jared woke up the next morning hung over. "Damn." He swung his feet to the floor and sat up squeezing his head. "That's the last time I drink spiced wine."

His eyes barely open, he brushed his fingers through his hair and looked around the room. In the corner were two boxes with his clothes heaped on top. "Oh yeah. I need to get those put away." Trying to stifle a belch as he reached for his pants, he smacked his lips at the bitter taste. "Ahhh, first things first."

Pulling a towel from under the pile of clothes, he tossed it over his shoulder and picked up his shower bag. "Now where did I put my toothbrush last night?" He looked in the bag. "Screw it. I'll find it later after breakfast."

Jared stumbled over to the door. Pulling it open, a paper tacked to the outside fluttered in his face. "Great, an eviction notice."

He ripped it down and blinked several times in an effort to focus his eyes on the handwritten note. "Clean the pool filter." He yawned. "Then the pool. Wash and paint pool furniture. Trim hedge along the patio. Keep an eye on Steven and Kris while they use the pool." Jared wadded the paper and threw it over his shoulder. "So now I'm a flippin' baby sitter, too?"

After his shower, dressed in shorts and t-shirt, he walked into the kitchen to fetch a cup of coffee. Spying Olga, the cook, putting things away in the pantry, Jared yelled out to her, "Good morning, Olga."

She looked over her shoulder at him and rolled her eyes, grunting an acknowledgment.

"And a good morning to you, my friend." Jared mimicked Shawn's greetings while he turned on the espresso machine. Searching through the cupboards for a large mug to pour it into, he blurted out, "Olga. Where's the.... ahh never mind, a beer stein will work."

He pulled the large clay stein from the back, then poured the first two shots in it. "Make it a double-double, barkeep. One for me, and one for my leettle frien'." Jared snickered as he pressed the switch on for a second batch.

INSIDE THE POOL SHED, Jared found wooden lounges stacked on edge, along with everything else he needed to do the chore list. Placing his coffee on the window sill, he began his conquest of the list. First he knelt next to the pool and shoved his hand in the water to get the filter basket. "Dang, that water's cold. I wonder if there is any way to heat it."

Rummaging around in the shed for a possible pool heater, he found the stereo connected to the speakers by the pool. "Well, well. This is going to make the day go faster."

Turning on the music, Jared proceeded to clean out the shed in an effort to find the control panel for the pool. As he grabbed the last wooden lounge chair, it seemed to be hung up on an opened patio umbrella. Jerking the lounger toward the shed door, the umbrella's rib broke and fell to the floor, uncovering the panel he was searching for. "Alright. I knew there had to be one." He shoved the chair out the door. "Now all I gotta do is figure out how to translate the labels and turn it on."

Unable to read the worn labels, he decided to go ahead and flip the two switches on the front. He smiled when a motor kicked on, along with the sound of a gas burner igniting. "OK,now to do the furniture until the water gets warmer."

He grabbed a can of paint and stepped outside to see Kris, wearing a string bikini, lying on one of the loungers. "You'll have to find someplace else, the pool's not open yet," he said as he set the can down.

"Early morning sun is the best time to tan. It's easier on the skin, don't you think?" Kris asked as she adjusted the lounger's back to lie flat. "Besides, you can take your time getting to this one."

"Dang," Jared grumbled as he went inside the shed to retrieve a bucket. "There goes the neighborhood."

Finished washing the other loungers, he stood next to Kris. "OK, I'm ready to do this one."

She turned her head and looked at the other chairs. "They're not painted."

"They have to dry."

Kris sat up and held out a bottle of sunscreen. "I'm dry, you can paint me."

"I'm doing the furniture." He dropped the bucket in his hand and went into the shed.

Finding a paintbrush, he looked out the door to see if she had left. Kris was lying face down while her swim top was floating in the pool. She shook the bottle of sunscreen and hollered, "Come put some on my back."

Jared stood in the doorway, picking at the brush. "No."

"Please."

He reached in the shed, grabbed his coffee from the window sill and took a drink. "No, put your top back on."

"Oooo." She stretched her arms above her head. "What are you afraid of?"

Setting the mug back on the sill, he retorted, "Nothing." Then snatching a smaller brush from its hook above the window, he bellowed out the door, "Especially you."

She raised up on her elbows with a sly grin. "Then why—"

Before she could argue any further, he reached down and grabbed the hose next to the door. "Put it back on or I'll cool you down."

"Oh alright." She pushed herself up off the lounger.

Wanting no temptation from the boss's niece, Jared spun around, stepped back into the shed and looked in a drawer, searching for something to open the paint can with. Pawing through the junk in the drawer, he faintly heard a splash and some garbled screeching. "Get out of the pool. I haven't cleaned it yet."

The noise continued for another minute then stopped. Jared looked out the window. Kris was floating face down in the cold water.

"Shi..." He slammed the drawer shut and ran to the pool. Jumping into the water next to her, he managed to drag her limp body out and onto the patio. He rolled her on her back and dropped onto his knees beside her.

She wasn't breathing.

Jared patted her face. "Come on, breathe. Damn it, don't do this to me." He sat back on his haunches and looked at her bare breasts for a moment. Hesitant to put his ear to her chest to hear a heartbeat, and since she didn't seem to be breathing, he decided instead to give her CPR. As he put his lips to hers, she instantly coiled her arms around his neck and shoved her tongue in his mouth.

Surprised, Jared struggled to pull away.

"Ahem!"

In his struggle to get free, he put a hand on one of her breasts as he pushed away in an effort to break her grip around his neck.

"Ahem!"

Kris winched and let go of him.

Jared sat back on his heels to see Angelina standing next to them. Wiping his mouth, he sputtered, "she fell in the pool—"

Kris sat up with a grin. "We were just getting acquainted."

Angelina glared at her. "So I see."

"It's not what you think." Jared got to his feet. "She was—"

"Having fun till you—" Kris picked up her top and stood looking at Jared. She reached out and touched the shattered bullet he kept on a chain around his neck. "That's an odd medallion."

He seized her wrist and snarled, "Don't touch."

Angelina glared at her. "Go in the house."

Jared let go of Kris.

She didn't budge.

Angelina folded her arms. Then squinting, she gave the half-naked teenager the evil eye.

Kris cattily brushed past Angelina. At the step to the house, she turned and winked at Jared then screeched, "grrrr-ow."

"Ooh that—"

Jared reached over, placing his hand on Angelina's shoulder. "You're—"

She twisted, brushing his hand off. "Don't touch me with the same hand you touched her with."

"Whoa!" Raising his hands up, he confessed, "I just wanted to say that you're right."

"What do you mean?" Angelina stepped away from him.

"You're right," He said, putting his hands on his hips. "The women in this family are dangerous," Jared glanced at the ground then into her eyes, "and I need you to protect me from them."

With a stern look on her face, Angelina stared back. Then with a slight twinge of a smile, she reached up, fingering the object hanging around Jared's neck. "What's significant about this?"

Jared wrapped his arms around her. "It's a reminder of my mortality."

She squeezed him back. "I don't get it."

He leaned back and pointed to the scar on his chest. "When the bullet hits the bone. . ."

Angelina softly touched the scar. "I'm sorry, I...I..."

Jared took hold of her hand. "I'm hungry. Shall we get something to eat?"

Chapter 16

Sitting at the kitchen table Jared watched Angelina put together a lunch for them. His cell phone's ringtone broke the silence. He rolled his eyes as he tugged at it to get it from his pocket. Laying it on the table he glanced at the caller ID; it was Marta.

He continued to watch her work while he silenced his phone.

Angelina trimmed the ends off several carrots and glanced over at him. "Who was that?"

Jared leaning on his elbows, flicked his phone in a circle. "Marta."

She gave him a wide-eyed look of disbelief. "Why didn't you answer it?"

"I'm with you," he said as he took a sip of coffee.

The phone rang again. She glanced over in time to see him push the phone away. Angelina gripped the counter and rolled her eyes. "Marta doesn't like that."

Undaunted, he took another sip. "I'll call her back after we eat."

The song started to play a third time.

"You better answer it with a good excuse."

"Fine." Picking up the phone, he hit the reject icon. As soon as the screen changed color, he tapped the redial icon. A busy signal emanated from the phone's speaker. Jared dropped his phone on the table. "It's busy."

"You're going to be sorry if you don't—"

Its song resumed playing once more.

Making a sour face, he rubbed his head with his fingertips, then snatched up the phone. "Hello? Yes ma'am. Sorry, I couldn't hear it ringing over the noise of the pool equipment. Anyway, how can I help you?"

Jared turned the speaker on and laid the phone on the table. "I need you to come to the office now, to deliver a car to Paris."

"Then where?"

"Back here to finish with the pool."

Jared waved his hand at Angelina and mouthed, "How'd she know?"

Putting a plate with vegetables and cold cuts on the table in front of him, Angelina shrugged.

Jared snapped his fingers and quipped, "Angie, want to go to Paris with me?"

"No," Marta objected through the phone.

"We could be back in time for you to go to work tomorrow."

"Yes!" Angelina squealed as she jerked the refrigerator door open.

"Absolutely not," Marta yelled. "You go alone. No passengers. No distractions. That's part of the job."

Jared sighed. "But she wouldn't be."

"I'm sending a taxi to pick you up."

"No!" Jared shook his head. "I need to eat and get cleaned up. I'll call one when I'm ready."

Marta could be heard tapping her fingernails on her desk. "You don't have time to eat. Paris needs this car now."

Angelina stood in front of the open refrigerator and shook a bottle of water above the door for Jared to see. He nodded. "Hey, I need to eat. I eat here, or in the car on the way. And most likely something will get spilled on the seat or floor."

The phone went silent. He tapped it. "Hello?"

"All right," Marta grumbled. "Make it fast. I need that car on the road."

"Yes ma'am." The screen changed colors before he finished. Jared glanced down at the phone. "She hung up."

Angelina sat across from him. "I can't believe she gave in that easy to you."

Jared gave her a whimsical smile and winked as he took an olive, popping it in his mouth.

"You think it's funny." She picked up a carrot stick and started to chew on it. "Marta's dangerous. Didn't Kristina just show you how menacing the women in this family can be?"

"Aren't you apart of the family?"

Angie stopped chewing, giving him a "how dare you" look.

He leaned across the table. "I've been in far worse situations than what these women can dish out." He batted his eyes several times. "It's you, I have to be careful of."

She straightened with a start. "What?"

With a serious expression, he pointed a finger at her. "It's you I need to worry about."

"Me?"

"Yes, you." He picked up a carrot and wagged it at her. "You could break my heart." He snapped the vegetable in two. "Chew it up..." he tossed a piece of it in his mouth, "and spit it out."

She sat there stone faced.

Jared grinned, then winked as he swallowed the carrot. She didn't change her expression. He picked up an olive and wrapped a piece of salami around it. "You didn't like that?"

She took a deep breathe then exhaled. "Are you saying I have that much power over you?"

Jared popped the food in his mouth. Then glanced around before he nodded.

Angelina slowly reached for the salt shaker on the end of the table. Sprinkling some in her hand, she held it up and blew the salt in Jared's direction.

He stiffened, his eyes glazed over.

She stretched out her hand shoulder high and jerked her index finger up and down.

Jared raised and lowered his right arm in unison with her finger. She wiggled her little finger. He did the same with his left arm. Angelina curled her hand, making a fist as Olga dropped a bag of groceries on the table.

The cook cleared her throat.

Angelina and Jared looked at her, then started laughing.

Olga smiled, but said nothing as she pulled a head of lettuce from the bag and put it in the refrigerator.

Angie spread her hands on the table and asked Jared, "So how long will you be gone?"

He picked up a breadstick and broke it. "I should be back tomorrow night."

"Call me this time."

Smearing some jam on the bread, he grinned. "What would you like me to call you?"

She sat up straight and pointed her nose in the air. "Your highness. Or maybe, master."

Olga choked as she tried to smother her giggling. The two looked over at her. Olga shoved the cloth shopping bag in a drawer. "I think that title has already been claimed by three others in this house."

Angelina drew an exasperated breath and eyed Jared.

He rose to his feet. "Yes, master. I will smear butter all over the insolent one and throw her in the oven."

Olga took a cookie out of the tin she had in her hands and waved it in front of Jared. "Careful, young man," she cackled, "don't think I haven't done this before."

Jared snatched the cookie from Olga's hand. "Sorry, Angie, she offered me a better deal."

Angelina blinked solemnly at him. "Promise me you'll call."

He kissed her on the cheek. "I promise."

"Thank you."

"I need to get ready." Grabbing several carrot sticks, he waved one at her. "But don't leave yet, I want to share the cab ride with you into the city."

Angelina began gathering the dishes. "OK."

Giving Angelina a thumbs up, Jared patted Olga on the shoulder as he left the kitchen.

"Are you going to keep him?" Olga asked, putting the kettle on the stove.

Angelina sat there, arms folded, chewing on her thumbnail. "I think so."

Chapter 17

It was late in the evening when Jared arrived in the Parisian industrial area. Yawning, he rubbed his tired eyes, while he waited for the leather-jacketed employee to open the gate. After he parked and shut the engine off, the man came alongside the car. Jared stepped out and handed him the envelope that went with the car.

"Merci," the man said, stuffing the envelope in his pocket.

"Is there someplace I can get a bite to eat before catching the train back?"

Sliding into the driver's seat, the man held out a business card, and pointed it down the street. "Five minutes that way. But call this number before you go to the train station."

Jared glanced at the card. "I already have Marta's number. I'll talk to her tomorrow when I get back to the office."

The man shoved it into Jared's hand. "Take the card." He closed the door and rolled the window down. Putting the car in gear, he looked at Jared. "Go eat, then do what you're told."

"Damn." Jared put the card in his jeans pocket. "What an attitude."

On the sidewalk outside the gate, he dialed Marta's number. "Hey, Marta. I just dropped off the car and am going to get something to eat before I head—"

"No!" she cut him off. "The agency in Greece needs a car that is there in Paris."

"You're kidding, nobody else has one closer?"

"It was a special order from the Peugeot factory."

"So..." Jared stopped and waited for a car to pass before crossing the street. "Why not ship it by train? There's less chance it'll get scratched."

"Not fast enough. It'll get hung up going through the half-dozen customs of the Balkan states. You'll need to take it into Italy and cross over by ferry to get it there in twenty-four hours."

"Impossible. Thirty-six max, and it'll cost you extra."

"Fair enough."

"Wait a minute..." Jared swung the cafe door open. "Why are you giving in so easy?"

"Get something to eat, then hurry back to the lot."

"You didn't answer my question."

"Jared, use your time wisely. Call her while you're eating." Marta's tone became snippy. "You don't need any distractions while you're driving for me."

"Yes ma'am."

Hanging up, he slipped into a chair and looked around the room. There were four people at a table on the other side of the dining room and no one else. *Good, it's quiet, I can call Angie.* He hit the speed dial for her number just as the waitress came alongside his table. Waiting for his call to connect, Jared looked up at the waitress. "A chicken dinner with a cup of coffee."

The call went through. "Yes?"

"Hey, Angie. It's me."

"Hi. Where are you?"

"I'm getting something to eat here in Paris before I head to Athens."

"Oh?" The phone went silent for a moment, then she asked, "Why are you going to Greece?"

"I don't know." Jared grabbed an ashtray from the next table. "I was told to call Marta when I got here. Aaand, she said they needed a brand new car delivered to the office in Athens."

"I knew she would pull something sneaky like that. Anything to win."

Jared glanced around to see if anyone heard her loud rant. "What are you talking about?"

"The festival at the club tomorrow night."

"Dang." He slapped his forehead. "I forgot all about that while I was talking to her."

"It doesn't matter. Sarina changed my schedule. I have to work every evening for the next two weeks."

The waitress quietly set a glass of water and his silverware in front of him. Jared smiled at her and asked in the phone, "What about Hans?"

"She cut Hans's hours in half. Then she barred him from showing up at her house. How is he supposed to get paid?"

"Hey, I'm sorry you got short-changed at work, but at least you're working. And I'm pretty sure Hans can make things work out, if he finds something else to do."

"He doesn't need the time off," Angelina harped. "He'll just spend it in one of those cafes."

"Just like you," Jared joked.

"Ha, ha, not funny. It took him two years to get his habit under control and motivated enough to get a job." Angelina's breath hissed in the phone. "And don't you be buying him any either."

Jared's thoughts flashed back to the day he met Hans. "Uhm, sure, OK."

The waitress walked by and set his coffee down. "Thank you," Jared offered her.

"For what?" Angelina asked.

"No, I was talking to..." Jared took the packet of sugar from the saucer under his cup, then pressing the phone to his shoulder with his ear, he dumped the sugar in his coffee. "To you. Thank you for being so understanding."

"How long are going to be gone?"

"A few days. Three there and the flight back." The waitress came back and placed Jared's supper before him. "Shouldn't be—" He looked up at the waitress. "This isn't what I ordered."

She pointed towards a man in a leather jacket, sitting on the other side of the restaurant.

It was the guy from the lot.

"Uhm, Angie, I have to go, something has just come up."

"Wait, what?"

Jared glanced at the steak platter. "I need to go. I'll call you later."

"Promise me you'll—"

Dropping the phone on the table, he picked up his knife and fork as the guy walked over and sat across from him. Jared took a bite of the steak. "Thanks for the dinner."

The guy leaned back in his chair. "It's on Marta. You have a long drive ahead of you and no time to stop."

"I would have been fine with the chicken." Jared took a bite of a breadstick.

"It wouldn't have be enough." The man replied as he twisted the tooth pick in his mouth. "I've had it before."

Jared put his elbows on the table and studied the bite of beef on the end of his fork. "Not bad. A little on the raw side for me."

The man sipped on the beer he brought with him. "No time to send it back. It'll have to do."

Jared stabbed at the pile of beets on his plate. "I thought I had more time."

"Nope. You need to finish and come back to the office." Reaching over and taking a piece of bread from the basket, the man insisted, "I have to give you directions how to get there."

"I think I can read a map."

"You have to stick to a special route to avoid getting bogged down in customs, or you'll miss the client in Athens."

Jared stopped chewing and watched the waitress serve a different customer. "What do mean? There are no customs checks inside the EU."

"You ask too many questions. It would be much easier to show you on the map back at the office." The leather-clad man looked at his watch. "Hurry up. You don't have much time. And we still have a lot to do."

"Then why don't you get started without me?"

"Can't." He drained the last of his beer. "Been told to make sure you don't get lost."

Taking a bite, Jared mumbled, "How? You're four blocks away."

"*Monsieur*," he pulled a fresh toothpick from his pocket. "I'm just doing my job. Don't make it difficult."

Jared took a drink of his coffee. Then picking up a piece of bread, wiped at the meat juices on his plate. "If you guys were doing your job, that car would have been on a train days ago. And delivered with no mileage on it."

"Oh, so now you have all the brains. Why didn't you tell this to the boss before she sent you all this way?"

Jared wolfed down the last of the food on his plate. "Sorry." He wiped his mouth. "It's just that I had to cancel a date with my girlfriend over that car."

"Ouch. Understandable, *monsieur*." The man looked at the glass entrance door. "But special orders are treated just that...special."

"I know. I know." Jared picked up his coffee and crooned, "Treat her like she's my girlfriend, 'cause she will be for the next week."

"Not what I meant." The guy waved to the waitress. Reaching under the counter, she brought over a thermos and two packets of sugar, setting them in front of Jared.

"What's this?"

"Espresso to help with your thirst." He leaned over the table and tapped the sugar packages. "Along with rocket fuel to help make it thru the long drive."

"Hmm." Jared picked up the sugar and stuffed them in his coat. "I'll need more than two. I like my coffee sweet."

Stone-faced, the guy shook his head and replied, "No you don't."

"Hey, I like my cof—"

The Frenchman stood up. "Time to go."

"Fine." Jared got to his feet. "Its not a problem. I'll pick some up at a rest stop."

Chapter 18

With sleep tugging at his eyelids, Jared approached the France-Italian border. He pulled into a fuel station rest stop and poured himself a cup of espresso from the thermos the Parisian waitress had given him. Setting the cup on the dash, he looked up Italy's highway information on his phone. "Mmmm, all I need is a toll sticker. OK. How much?" Scrolling through the data, he reached for the coffee and took a sip. As it covered his tongue, he struggled to swallow the small amount in his mouth. "Man, that is bitter."

He looked through the brown bag on the passenger seat for something sweet to put in it. "Ahhh, dang it. I forgot to pick up some sugar. No, wait a minute. I got those two packs some...where. Yep, there they are. In the ashtray where I put them."

Jared ripped one open and dumped it in the cup. Hesitant with the second pack, he thought, *There's another cup in the thermos. Maybe I better hang onto it one until I've picked up more.*

Stepping out of the car, he set his coffee and phone on the vehicle's roof then shoved a cigarette in his mouth. After lighting it, he picked up his phone. "Let's see, twenty-five euros for a toll sticker. Not too bad. Now to figure a route." He took a drink of coffee as the map bounced around the screen on his phone. "Damn," he fought to keep from spitting it out, "a mud puddle tastes better than this crap. I sure hope they have something better inside the station." He locked the car door, then glanced at his cell phone for the time. "Alright, Angie should still be up."

Jared dialed her number, and walked toward the station waiting for her to answer.

ANGELINA, WALKING TO the platforms in Amsterdam's Central train station, took a deep breathe as she looked for her train. Once on the train, she slipped into her seat and softly sang along with the Whitney Houston song, I Will Always Love You, as it came thru the car's public address system. By the end of the song she wiped away a tear and watched the station platform slip by.

GETTING NO ANSWER, Jared strolled through the store and grabbed a sandwich, two bottles of water, and a box of sugar cubes. He set them on the counter. "I need a toll sticker too, please."

The clerk set the sticker on the counter.

Jared's hand started to tremble as he tried to put his card in the payment slot. Carefully, with two hands, he managed to get it in place. His fingers now shaking uncontrollably, he fumbled with the number pad. It took three tries to get the pin number entered right.

"You OK?" the clerk asked.

"Yeah, just tired and hungry."

Holding out the the receipt, the clerk pointed towards the door. "There's a hotel across the lot. Don't drive if you're sleepy."

Gathering his items, Jared took the paper from the clerk. "Thanks, I'll take a nap in my car."

When he got to the car, his were hands shaking so much he couldn't hold the key fob still long enough to push the button. Setting the bag of food on the ground, he tried using two hands to hold the key still long enough get it into the door lock without scratching the car. "Oh man, get it open and sit down."

He couldn't stop shaking. Taking a deep breath and holding it, he tried to push the fob button once more; the door clicked.

Jerking the door open he sat on the edge of the seat and scarfed the sandwich down, making an effort not to get bread crumbs in the car. Finished, he guzzled an entire bottle of water. Gasping for breath, Jared wiped his mouth with his sleeve and stepped away from the car before lighting a cigarette. "Damn, that was some caffeine rush. No wonder the Frenchman called it rocket fuel."

With the toll sticker in place in the window, Jared started the car and punched the accelerator. Alone on the motorway and unable to sit still, he fiddled with the stereo controls on the steering wheel, volume, time, bass, channel,volume, channel.... Flying down the highway, time quickly melted away along with the miles.

Outside of Florence, he stopped to take a short break and buy fuel. His head still going a million miles an hour as the petrol flowed into the gas tank, he stared at his phone, searching for the ferry's website.

Finding the site in Italian, presented a bit of a problem in his effort to maneuver to the schedules page. But just as the pump clicked off, it popped up. Jared hung up the hose and jumped in. He pulled the car over into the parking lot and shut the engine off, then snatched up his phone again. The page showed each of the Adriatic seaport's schedules. "Lets see... if I jump on the one just out of Florence, it'd take twenty hours. Too long. That'll put me four hours over. What else is there?" Rolling down the window, he sucked in a deep breath of the cool night air, then swiped at the screen. "If I go out of Brindisi. It would be... a six hour drive. Plus eight on the boat. I could make it. Just barely."

He poured the last swallow of the espresso in the thermos into his cup and dropped two cubes of sugar into it. Swirling the coffee as the sugar dissolved, he added a little water to thin the mixture out. Raring to go with just one sip, Jared swung back on the motorway.

AT THE FERRY TERMINAL in Brindisi, Jared parked the car on board and got out. Feeling like he's dragging a heavy iron chain behind him as he climbed the stairway to the deck, he decided to visit the cafeteria before finding a lounge chair to sleep on.

With a bag of chips and soda in hand, he leaned back in the lounge chair. After eating a few chips, he tried Angelina's number once more.

It rang twice, then he heard, "Sor... mailbo...ull...umber—"

"Dang, I thought these ships were suppose to have better reception. Maybe I can get hold of Hans."

Hans didn't answer his phone, either.

ANGELINA WALKED OUT of the train station and spotted a familiar car. She briskly walked over to it and handed her bags to an older, rough looking man. He put them in the trunk of his car, closed the lid and gave her a hug. "I've missed you."

She hugged him back. "I've missed you, too."

He smiled as he gazed into her eyes, then nodded. The two quietly got into the car and sped off.

JARED'S ALARM WENT off an hour before the ferry was to dock. Getting up, he went inside to the cafeteria and dished up breakfast from the buffet. After setting his tray down on a table, he took a handful of sugar cubes from his pocket and dumped them into his coffee. He then stabbed at some scrambled egg with his fork and popped it into his mouth. First swirling his coffee under his nose to make sure the sugar was dissolved, he then washed the mouthful of egg down with the sweetened concoction and sighed, "Ahh, that's more like it. I need to get rid of the last of that bitter crap in the car."

On his way out, Jared stopped by the counter and bought a large to-go cup of coffee to take with him. At the car he settled into the driver's seat and blew on the steaming coffee. A few hot drops hit his hand causing him to set the cup in the cup holder. "Oow, wait a minute. If I spill this, Marta's gonna get really pissed." Opening the thermos, he looked in. "There might be a half cup left. Let's see...how am I going to do this without...?" Holding the cup and thermos out the window, he managed to avoid burning his fingers pouring from one to the other.

Done, he set the empty cup in the cup holder and picked up the thermos cap. The car in front of him lurched and pulled forward toward the ramp off the ferry. Jared quickly screwed the cap back on the vacuum bottle and flung it on the floor as he punched the accelerator, barely missing the crewman directing vehicles.

Away from the port, on the motorway to Athens, Jared poured a drink from the thermos back into the cup. The bitter smell of the mixed coffees curled his nose. Looking around the car for the box of sugar cubes while keeping an eye on the road, he couldn't find them. Not wanting to stop, he felt his pockets hoping he might still have a few of the cubes left in one from breakfast. Instead he found the second sugar packet the Frenchman had given him. Jared held it up for inspection. "What the heck? I thought I used both. Oh well, sugar is sugar." He poured the bag into his mouth. Choking on the gritty, odd taste it had, he quickly tossed back a mouthful of coffee. The sugar stuck to his throat.

Gagging and huffing in an effort to breathe and not to spew the sticky mixture all over the dash, he whipped the car to the side of the road and bailed out. Hitting the ground, he swallowed what was in his mouth. "Damn," he coughed. "You're a stupid fool. You could have wrecked. Man that was not what I expected." Jared leaned against the door and took another drink of coffee. "Dang, bit-it-it-ter. I ain't gonna taste a thing for a week." He wagged his tongue trying to get rid of the taste as he set the coffee cup on the ground then reached in the car for his phone.

He saw that his hands were shaking again as he tried to dial and could feel his heart racing like the night before when he bought the toll sticker. Jared climbed in behind the wheel and took several deep breaths trying to relax. "No more coffee, just get this damn car delivered."

He looked in the mirror; the road was clear. Punching it, the open door slammed shut as the car rocketed to 120 KPH were he held it.

On the outskirts of Athens, Jared googled the address the Frenchman had given him. Frustrated and unable to read the Greek letters in the directions, he threw his phone across the car. Closing his eyes only for a second, he opened them in time to swerve, missing the truck that had changed lanes in front of him. He pounded on the steering wheel, honking, as he flew by the slower truck.

A petrol sign ahead snagged his attention.

Whipping into the station, he jumped out of the car and ran in. Finding a city map, he unfolded it on the counter and asked the clerk to mark his route.

He arrived at the lot a half hour late. The lot manager fumed as Jared stepped out of the car, "I'm not going to give you the papers until we inspect the car. I want to make sure it isn't damaged."

Jared sat on a stool in the service bay. "Not a problem. I'll just sit here and watch."

"You'll be in the way," the manager sneered. "Why don't you go in the office and wait."

"Sorry." Jared pulled out a cigarette. "There's nothing wrong with that car. You're not going to screw me out of my pay."

The manager turned away. "This isn't about you." He motioned at the two mechanics standing by their toolboxes and nodded toward Jared. They grabbed his arms and ushered him to the office.

An hour later, with the delivery papers, his money, and plane reservation in hand, Jared walked past the garage on his way to the gate.

He stopped at the shop door in time to see one of the mechanics pull a package from behind the headliner of the car he had just brought in.

Biting his lip, he walked out to the cab waiting for him.

Chapter 19

Landing in Amsterdam from Athens with a double layover, it was in the middle of the afternoon when Jared walked into Marta's office. He tossed the envelopes from his deliveries onto her desk and flopped down on her couch. "There's your paperwork," he said and leaned back.

Marta opened one of the brown envelopes and rubbed the inside of the flap with a wet finger. "Any problems I need to know about?"

He sat up. "You know they ripped that car apart and repainted it?"

"The client specified a special color." She reached into her open safe, pulling out a bundle of euros. "And the factory didn't have that color. Here...I need another Porsche taken to Frankfurt tonight."

"You'll have to find someone else." Jared leaned back and shut his eyes. "I need some sleep."

She reached into the safe and pulled out another stack of bills. Marta laid the second one on top of the first. "Double, if you'll do it."

"I don't know. I'm pretty tired and another eight hours..."

Marta poured him a cup of coffee. She took a packet of sugar from her desk and dropped it into the coffee. "Here, think about it while I finish with these papers."

Jared watched the paper wrapper slowly disappear. His stomach rumbled loud enough for Marta to hear. She reached into her drawer and tossed a granola bar beside the cup. He picked it up and curiously inspected the wrapper.

Watching him through her peripheral vision, Marta asked, "Is there a problem with it?"

"I saw the package in the headliner..." he took a sip of his coffee. "And I—"

"A big flat package?"

He nodded. "Wrapped in plastic."

"That was their monthly pay."

Jared swirled his cup looking for the paper sugar packet Marta had dropped in the coffee. Glancing up at her, he asked, "Is that why you're paying me cash upfront?"

"We don't believe in banks. They will steal your money if you're not careful."

Jared snorted at her comment as he swirled the coffee again. "Where's the paper wrapper?"

Marta grabbed a second granola bar, walked around the desk and leaned against the edge of it. Holding the bar out to Jared, she ignored his question and offered, "It's more like avoiding being taxed in both countries: twenty-two percent by the Dutch and twenty-four percent by the Greeks." She picked up the bundles of money next to her and waved them back and forth. "If you want, I can pay both the Dutch and the German tax on this job."

"No," he shot back, wide awake after finishing the coffee. Rising to his feet, he gently pulled the money from her grip. "But when I get back, I want a couple of days off."

"Fair enough." She handed him a business card. "Here's the number. You know the drill."

"Can I get another coffee to go?"

Marta poured him another cup and set a packet from her desk beside it while he dialed Angelina's number. "One ringy-dingy...two ringy...hello?" He stepped out of the office. "Angelina—"

"Jared!"

"It's me. I was call—"

"I'm not in Amsterdam anymore. I can't...stop it, Peter. Don't. Jared, I'm busy at the moment and can't talk." She hung up.

Jared reared back to throw the phone. Marta grabbed his wrist. "Don't. You'll need it tonight."

ANGELINA WHISPERED, "Come on, Hans, answer your phone," as she waited for him to answer. Finally she heard a click and then music in the background. "Hans? Hans?"

"Yes?"

"I'm here with father."

"What? Father is in Amsterdam?"

"No. I'm in Spain with him. I didn't want you to worry." Angelina leaned over the coffee table rubbing her head as she spoke. "I was beginning to fall in love with him."

"So?"

"You know I can't. He's not one of us. I couldn't do it to him. So I came home."

"Does Jare...what?"

"As the responsible family member for me, you should have stepped between us."

"That is old custom, Angie. You know we don't follow it no more."

"As the son, you may not have to, but as a daughter, I have to."

"What? Not...when did...does Jared know you are gone?"

Angelina shook her fist when she heard his question and sniped, "Chasing cars has become his new love." Leaning back on the couch, she let out a big sigh. "Anyway, I'm not sure I want him to know."

"Is not fair, Angie. He is just trying to cope. Like fathe—."

"That's not true. And don't you compare him to our father." She wiped her eyes with her sleeve. "Besides, he could have found someone else."

"No. You asked him out, remember?"

"Don't pin that one on me. We," she jerked her arm back and forth as if she were pointing at the both of them, "have to stick with the family. He doesn't!"

"Angie. He is a part of family. Just a different part."

"Then why doesn't he follow our traditions?"

"What? What are you really mad about?"

Shaking her head, Angelina whined, "I'm not mad." Exasperated, she looked up at the ceiling. "It's not fair. Not after seeing what father had to go through."

"Ahh, I get it. You are afraid of loving him."

"That's not—" Angelina's phone dropped the call. "Hans? Are you there?" Tossing her phone on the couch, she crossed her arms and closed her eyes.

JARED ARRIVED AT THE Frankfurt yard ten minutes before midnight. He parked the car at the edge of the lot and shut it off. Looking around, he dialed the number on the card. His phone rang twice, then went silent. He could hear a radio coming through it in the background. Jared tartly murmured into his phone, "I'm here. Slot 7 B."

Hanging up, he gathered the delivery papers along with his coat. As he walked across the lot meeting the attendant in the middle, he slapped the keys and paperwork against the guy's chest. "Talk to you next time. I got a train to hop."

A block from the train station, his phone rang. "Oh great, Marta! Now what?" Grimacing, he pushed the green icon. "Yes?"

"You left a package at the yard, go get it."

"I'll miss my train."

"It'll come out of your pay if they have to ship it."

"What! You—" *Click.* Jared looked at his phone; the screen was blank. "Damn that woman."

Grudgingly, he turned around. The attendant met him at the door with the package in his hands. "Don't be in a such a hurry next time."

"Hey, the next train doesn't leave for another two hours and I didn't feel like hanging around all night."

"There's a couch over there. Just don't expect me to wake you up."

"Whatever," Jared growled, and slumped on the office couch.

From where Jared sat, he could see into the repair shop. He watched as the car he just delivered, was torn apart and small bundles were pulled from their hiding spots. After they were done and started to put the car back together, he stared at the package in his hands, for a moment he didn't know what to think. "Damned if I do, damned if I don't," he fumed getting off the couch. Walking over to the receptionist's desk, he plucked a piece of candy from a dish on it before going out the door.

Finding the train and alone in a compartment, he put Marta's package inside his coat and zipped it up to his chin. Then folding his arms over the package he watched the station slip away into the darkness. He soon fell asleep with the movement of the train.

An unfamiliar odor roused him from his slumber. His warrior instincts told him to open his eyes slowly. Through narrow slits, he could see a hand making an effort to unzip his coat.

Suddenly his thoughts flashed back to Afghanistan and how the Taliban booby-trapped the unsuspecting.

Jared seized the hand on his zipper and punched its hooded owner in the face multiple times. As the insurgent tried to pull away, he jumped to his feet threw the enemy headfirst into the compartment's wall.

The hooded figure, coughing and spitting blood, rose from the floor onto their hands and knees. Jared kicked the choking body up onto the compartment seat, where it rolled onto its back and the hoodie fell away. With his fist drawn back to strike again, Jared quickly blinked in an attempt to clear his hazy vision and then saw it was a woman's bloody face, not a bearded insurgent.

"Damn it, woman." He wiped the sweat from his forehead with his sleeve. "I nearly killed you."

She didn't blink.

He took a closer look at her. She didn't seem to be breathing. He put his fingers on her throat to check for a pulse, It was then, he caught the faint click of a knife blade locking in the open position. Quickly pinning her hand against the seat with his knee, he jerked on a fist full of her hair and glared into her glassy eyes. "Drop it! Or I'll snap your scrawny neck."

She dropped the knife.

Jared stood up, keeping an eye on her while he slid the compartment door open. Glancing both ways down the corridor, he stepped from the compartment and briskly walked toward the end of the train. He entered the last car as the train slowed for its next stop. Not sure if the woman would run to a conductor or to the Dutch police, Jared feared for the worst and bailed off the train running for the station's exit. Outside the small rural station, he hid in the bushes. Waiting until he felt it was safe, he called a taxi.

The cab took him directly to Marta's office. Stomping in, Jared tossed the brown-paper package in front of her. "Your precious almost got stolen on the train."

"Oh?"

"That's not the worst of it. I almost killed the woman trying to steal it."

Marta tore the wrapper off the package. She held up the box of sugar packets inspecting its cellophane wrapper. "Good thing you didn't. I'd have to turn you in."

Jared slapped the delivery envelope on her desk. "I wasn't joking." He glared at the brightly colored box in her hand as she mulled over it. "You had me miss my train for a box of sugar?"

"Not just any sugar. This is something new." Marta put the box in her drawer. "And can only be bought in Frankfurt."

"Pfft. You can buy that brand down the street."

Picking up the envelope, Marta glanced at it, then at him. "I need you to drive—"

"No." He lit a cigarette. "I'm tired and I want to see Angelina."

"She's not here anymore. I need you—"

"What do you mean, *not here*?"

Marta opened the envelope and wet the inside of the flap. "She quit and left while you were in Greece."

Jared spun around and ran out the door. Out on the sidewalk, he dialed Angie's number.

No answer.

He dialed Hans. "Come on, Hans, answer...please."

"Hello?"

"Hans, it's me Jared. What's this I hear? Angelina left? Where did she go? Did she say where? I mean...why?"

"Don't worry, comrade. She said she need a holiday, and—"

"Where? For how long? Did she say anything?"

"No, no, and no. I will say, she has trouble to work out. And would be wise to leave her alone for a while. Comrade, I need to work. Come by boat and we'll talk."

"Yeah, sure." Jared hung up. "Talk to you later," he mumbled as he shoved the phone in his pocket. Stomping back inside, he held out his hand. "Gimme the damn keys, I'll drive."

"Not like that, you won't." Marta held out a card-lock key. "Go in back and get cleaned up, then rest your heels on that couch until the car is ready."

Several hours later, Marta came into the office and nudged him. "Here, you'll need this."

"What?" Jared opened his eyes to see the coffee in Marta hands. "Thanks."

She walked around her desk and sat in her chair. "The car will be ready in a few minutes."

Jared fingered the packet of sugar she placed on the saucer and asked, "What's so special with this brand?"

Marta took four more packs from her desk drawer and gently fingered them. "It's certified organic and—"

He tore the one open. "What isn't anymore?"

She set the four in her hand on the corner of her desk. "The paper is made from sugar and dissolves in the beverage. No waste. No garbage." Leaning back, she folded her arms. "Need I say more?"

"Oh brother. The three R thing. Should have known." Jared dropped the empty wrapper in his coffee and watched it dissolve. "So where am I going?"

"Bremerhaven. From there you'll go to Prague. Then to Marseilles, where you'll return by train." She picked up a waist pack from the floor and tossed it to Jared. "Here, I suggest you put the envelopes in this before you board the train."

"A fannie pack! Good idea. Never would have thought of it." He rose to his feet and downed the coffee that was left in his cup, then placing it on her desk, he snickered, "With the French Riviera being the last stop, I should be back, say...in a week."

"You have four days."

He lit a cigarette. "That's really pushing it. I figure I'll need at least eighteen hours of sleep during that time."

Pointing to the sugar on the corner of her desk, Marta retorted, "You'll make it with that in your coffee."

Jared picked up the packets and looked at them. Shoving them in his shirt pocket, he hooted, "Yeah, right."

"Don't get them damp," she commanded as she held out the keys.

He pointed his finger at her and demanded, "I want a couples of days off when I get back."

"Sure." Marta reached out, grabbed his finger and shook it. "Just keep the sugar dry so it doesn't melt in your pocket."

Chapter 20

Everything went as planned for the delivery in Bremerhaven. Then the road to Prague was empty and Jared arrived early. Having never showed up early before, he was adamant about keeping ahead of schedule and pressed the people in Prague to speed up the prep of his next car.

Three hours still on the upside, Jared jumped into the dark blue Land Rover and pointed it down the autobahn toward Austria. The SUV handled smoothly as he pressed the accelerator to the floor.

Deep in the Austrian Alps, Jared looked up at the rugged peaks. "Wow, just as steep and barren as those in Afgha—" He saw a helicopter hovering over a patch of trees on one of the hillsides. Focusing his attention on it, as his eyes began to flit back and forth between the chopper and the highway, he unconsciously muttered, "Dave, keep an eye out for IED's."

No sooner had the words left his mouth, than a raven swooped in front of the SUV. Jared slammed on the brakes and jerked the wheel to the right. The SUV skidded across the pavement and down into the ditch. He baled out as the Land Rover's bumper came to rest against a mud embankment. Kneeling, he scanned the area while blindly feeling around for his rifle. "Dave, you see anything? Dave? Dave?"

Pivoting to see why Dave wasn't answering, Jared stared through the open door into the Land Rover. "Dave?" He rose to his feet, staring at Dave in the passenger seat with blood oozing from multiple wounds.

"It's not your fault, Jared." Dave took a deep breath. "I never was very lucky."

Pawing under the driver's seat, Jared felt around for a first aid kit. "Damn it, Dave, don't—"

Dave stared down at his chest. "Then again, I cheated the reaper. Not one bullet hit a bone."

A hand touched Jared's shoulder. "Hey! You OK?"

"Call a medic, Dave's hit pretty bad," Jared yelled as he turned to face the stranger.

"Who?" the stranger asked.

"Dave!" Jared spun back around facing the SUV and saw that Dave had disappeared. Stunned, he stared at the empty seat.

"Are you OK? Should I call an ambulance?"

"I'm OK." He patted the stranger on the shoulder. "Something ran in front of me and I tried to miss it." Exhaling a deep breath, Jared offered, "Thank you for stopping," and held out a cigarette to the man. After he lit both of their cigarettes, Jared climbed into the Land Rover. "If you don't mind, I'm on a time schedule."

The stranger walked back to his car, shaking his head as Jared four-wheeled the SUV out of the ditch, throwing mud everywhere.

ON THE FRENCH SIDE of the Alps, Jared pulled into a fuel station that had a self-serve car wash. Plugging a handful of euros in the coin slot, he washed every inch of the dirty vehicle, then filled it with petrol and got back onto the autobahn. Plucking his coffee cup from the cup-holder, he glanced inside. "Empty. Damn, I need..." he crushed the cup and threw it on the floor next to a bottle of water, "I need something." He felt his shirt pocket for his cigarettes and found the two remaining sugar packages. "Who needs coffee with this stuff."

He pulled over to the side of the autobahn and picked up the water. Twisting its top off, he took a swig then set the bottle in the cup holder.

"Now for the sweet stuff." Jared tore open a packet and started to pour it into the narrow-necked water bottle when he stopped, looked at the package, then shoved it wrapper and all in his mouth. Puckering, he ground his teeth and tried not to spit out the bitter surprise. Snatching up the water bottle, he chugged it in an attempt to wash what he could down his throat. "Damn! What the...whoo, whee, bitter." Holding up the last packet, he studied it. "Organic, schmanic. Somebody took some time cookin' up this idea."

The warm euphoric rush came quickly with no caffeine to blame it on. His heart pounded. Jared at that point could no longer deny his suspicion of what his job really was about. Angry, he tossed the last small envelope on the passenger seat and stomped on the accelerator, leaving black streaks on the pavement as he tried to merge into fast moving traffic. "Settle down man, settle down. You'll never see her again if you kill yourself."

During the thoughtless maneuver his thumb, had bumped the radio button on the steering wheel. The radio's static noise soothed his self-condemning thoughts. The more he heard, the more he relaxed and continued pushing the tuning button until a song in English came on. It was John Prine singing his song about Sam Stone. A wounded Vietnam Vet who came home addicted to morphine.

Jared's eyes misted as he listened to the words. When he heard the reference about the monkey on Sam's back and where all his money went, Jared turned the radio off. After several cigarettes, he reached over and picked up the last sugar packet from the seat. The paper envelope stuck to his fingers as he rolled it around between thumb and finger.

He decided he didn't need crystal meth and to get rid of it. But each time he tried to throw it out the window, the *sugar packet* squealed like a monkey and stuck to his fingers. Eventually, the monkey won the tug-of-war and Jared placed the sugar in his shirt pocket, next to the shattered bullet he wore on the chain around his neck.

Arriving at the lot in Marseilles still three hours ahead of schedule, he eased the SUV onto the lot. The manager ran out and stopped Jared. "Take the car somewhere else until it's time."

Jared shoved his door open, pushing the manager back. "Give me my envelope. I got a train to catch."

The manager looked at the broken turn signal lens. "You've damaged the vehicle. I'll have to inspect it before I can give you the papers."

"Well then? Get to it."

"There are others cars ahead of you." The manager tugged on the sleeves of his leather jacket. "I won't be able to inspect it for another three hours. Take it off the lot and tour the city until then."

Jared grabbed the manager's hand and slapped the keys in his palm. "I'm tired. You take it for a spin. I'll be on the couch in your office."

The manager climbed in the Land Rover. "Hey, it smells like smoke in here, we'll have—"

Jared, raising his middle finger above his head, continued to walk towards the office.

ANGELINA SAT AT THE piano playing a children's melody, as she watched her father place their students about on the stage. Without much thought, the music she was playing subtly changed to the Beth Hart song that had become stuck in her head. At first, she mumbled the words to, *Spanish Lullabies*, but the more she played, the louder she sang.

"Angie," her father cleared his throat, "I love your voice, but please stay focused."

"Sorry, it's just—"

"We'll talk about him later, OK? I promise."

She nodded and started the children's song over again.

ARRIVING BACK IN AMSTERDAM, Jared walked into Marta's office and tossed the envelopes on her desk. "Here. Now if you don't mind, I'm going home to sleep and get cleaned up."

"No. Sit down until I've opened them."

"You don't need me for that. Besides we agreed—"

"We agreed you wouldn't smoke in the cars. Detailing is an added expense."

"Gimme a break, it's not like—"

Marta looked up at him. "Like what? Wrecking an eighty thousand euro Land Rover?"

Jared sucked in a deep breath through his teeth. "Yeah, that." Dropping onto the couch, he rubbed his face. "That was either luck or stupidity."

Marta got up and went to the refrigerator. Pulling out a bottle of apple juice she opened it and poured two tablets from her hand into the bottle. Closing the refrigerator door, she walked around the desk to Jared. "Here. No more coffee."

"What?" He looked up at her through bloodshot eyes.

"It'll be a few more minutes. You can have this till I'm done."

Jared downed half the bottle, then took out a cigarette.

Marta glanced over at him and then pushed an ashtray in his direction.

But before he could find his lighter, his eyes were closed.

ANGELINA SET HER FATHER'S coffee in front of him and sat down across the table. "How could he, after I warned him? Even Hans..." She looked away and bit her lip.

He brushed his thick, jet-black mustache and listened to her rant. After she stopped, he put his hand on hers. "My dear, I warned you about your mother's cousins. But you still went."

"It's not the same. As a soldier he should have sensed the—"

"As a soldier, he has been trained to take responsibility, regardless of the danger."

Angelina picked up her cup and looked at her father. She weakly smiled. "You're right. I wish I could have heard it from mother, though."

"I wish you could have too." Her father set his cup down and took a deep breath. "I wish I had not gone off to Afghanistan. Then your mother might still be alive to tell you."

"Brezhnev could have learned how to be more vile from those two." She spit on the ground. "He should have sent the two of them, then Russia would have won."

"Don't go there, Angie. The bitterness will turn you into an empty shell and eventually consume your soul." He reached up and rubbed the locket hanging around his neck. "I think your mother would agree with me. When I came back, I was numb from all the death that had happened in front of me. But your mother's... hers nearly killed me. Had it not been for Christ's love and the many prayers," he closed his eyes, "I would not have been able to raise you and Hans."

Angelina rose to her feet and put her arms around her father's neck. "You did the best you could."

He reached up and touched her face. "Be patient, he's been to hell, and a piece of it is still buried in him. I sense God's not done with him yet. Shall we light a candle for him at mass this afternoon?"

Angie sat back down, wiped her eyes, and nodded.

Chapter 21

Jared opened his eyes. The familiar ceiling of his room stared back at him. "Ahh, damn. How did I get here?" While he laid in bed trying to rub his massive headache away with both hands, a third arm slid from under the covers and across his chest.

Turning his head, he looked to see who the arm belonged to. Surprised, he leaped up from the bed, grabbed his pants and a towel, then raced out the door to the bathroom.

In the shower he let the water run over his head as he tried to guess how she ended up in his bed. The hot water began to run out before he could remember anything of what happened after showing up at Marta's office. He wrapped his towel around his waist, stepped out of the shower stall and stood in front of a sink, staring at himself in the mirror.

Kris walked in the bathroom with just her panties on, and nonchalantly started to brush her teeth in the sink next to him.

After a long silence, Jared turned and leaned against the sink's edge. "Look... don't get any idea that just because we slept together, that... that—"

"What?" She looked at him in the mirror. "That you can have your way with me anytime you want?"

"No." He cradled his head in his hand.

"That I get what I want?"

"No! Because of your mother—"

Kris spit in the sink. "My mother doesn't control me."

"Well, your aunt does me," he retorted. "And I don't want her to have a reason to fire me."

She leaned close to the mirror and inspected her teeth. "Marta doesn't need a reason."

"That's not the point. I don't want to lose Angelina."

Kris turned, wrapped her arms around him, and laid her head on his shoulder as she cooed, "But I want you."

He reached for her wrists as he blurted out, "No."

She immediately shoved him away. "You're dumber than I thought."

"What?"

She snatched up her toothpaste and brush. "Think about it, stupid."

Jared rolled his eyes. "Cat and mouse."

She sauntered toward the door. "I can have anyone that I want." Opening it, she turned. "Besides, I made sure Angelina isn't around anymore."

Jared grabbed the wooden-handle scrub brush from under the sink and threw it at her as she let the door swing shut.

JARED'S PHONE RANG as he downed the last swallow of his beer. Dropping the bottle in the wheelbarrow full of weeds and trimmings, he answered it, "Yes?"

"It's Marta. I need you to come to the office, there's a cab on its way."

"OK. Where am I going to?"

"You'll find out when you get here."

"OK. How long will—"

"You'll find out when you get here."

Lighting a cigarette, Jared asked, "Do I need to pack anything?"

"You'll find—"

"Yeah, yeah, I'll find out when I get there. I'll need to eat and grab a cup of coffee."

"You can do that when—"

"Hold on, someone is beeping in."

"No! Don't—"

Jared looked at his phone, then switched lines. "Angie! I've been trying to get hold of you all week, but it keeps going to voicemail."

"I know." Angelina's voice was very soft. "I needed time to think."

"About what?"

"About us. I...I wasn't—"

Suddenly the phone was ripped from his hand and flung into the pool by Kris. "The cab is here and Aunt Marta wants you, *now*."

Jared raised his hand to backhand her. Thinking better of it, he lowered his hand and growled, "That was Angelina." Rolling his fingers into a fist and popping his knuckles, he saw the skimmer net propped against one of the chairs. "That was really brilliant of you," he snapped, as he grabbed it and fished his phone out of the pool. "Now how am I going to stay in contact with your aunt?"

"She has a spare at the office," Kris sniped at him and folded her arms. "The cab is waiting."

"Watch it." He shook the phone hard. "You don't tell me what to do."

"As long as you work for the family I do."

"Stuff it, little girl. I... " Jared pulled the rubber cover off his phone. "I work for your aunt, not you."

Kris grabbed her shirt as if to tear it. "What do you think she'll say if I tell her what you did to me last night?"

Shoving his phone into his back pocket, Jared snorted, "Go ahead. I doubt she'll believe you." He started to walk away.

She stepped in front of him and put her hands around her throat. "When she asks why I'm crying and I show her these marks...you're dead meat."

"Whoa, whoa. You wouldn't dare?"

Kris smiled. "Try me."

"OK, you win." He held out his hand. "Truce. OK?"

She looked at his hand. Smiling, she reached out to shake it.

Jared snatched her wrist. Jerking her off her feet, he threw her in the pool. As she came to the surface, he shook his finger at her. "Stay away from me, or you'll be treading something worse than water."

JARED SHOOK HIS PHONE one more time as he stepped from the cab. Upset that it still didn't work, he flung the front door open and went into Marta's office. Without looking up from her work, Marta asked, "You ever ride a motorcycle?"

"Yes." He stuffed the phone in his back pocket. "When I was younger I used to ride motocross and dirt track racing, why?"

"I need a motorcycle in Bratislava brought here."

Jared dropped onto the couch. "I assume there'll be other deliveries included."

She peeked over the paper in her hand at him. "There'll be other cars to deliver, yes."

He pulled out a cigarette and fidgeted with it. "That's not what I meant."

Marta leaned back in her chair, twirling the pen in her hand. "What do you mean?"

Flicking his Zippo lighter open and striking it, the flame danced inches from the end of his cigarette. "I mean, there'll be other packages in the cars, right?"

"What are you talking about?" She turned, took a cup and filled it with coffee from the carafe on the counter behind her. "I've told you before... that some of the cars carry payroll." Marta placed a packet of sugar from her desk drawer on the cup's saucer and slid it toward him. "I shouldn't have to explain. If you're stopped, the less you know, the less chance you'll get arrested. And the less chance the money becomes tied up in a legal battle."

"Don't play with me." He took a drag, "I know what is with the sugar."

"Are you saying something about my brother's business? If you are—"

"Look," he tossed the packet back across the desk, then picked up the cup. "I don't mind carrying the payroll, but I ain't running no drugs."

Marta flipped the packet with her pen. "Is one of the managers doing something on the side I don't know about?"

"You know what..." Jared shook his head. "How shall I put it?"

She leaned back. "With care."

"You know what? I need a new phone." He took another puff and pointed at her. "Your niece threw mine in the pool."

Marta pulled an old flip phone from her desk and tossed it to him. "I'll have a talk with her."

"You do that. Are all the numbers I need, in it?"

She slid a business card across her desk. "Call me when you get there." Sitting back, Marta bit her lower lip and stared at him. He stared back. Slowly she smiled, then offered, "While you're there, consider asking the manager about where to buy a replacement phone. I hear you can get some really good deals in Bratislava."

Jared picked up the card. "If we're done with business, you said you'd have everything I need here."

She hesitated to answer him as she played with the top button of her blouse, finally she quipped, "So I did." Pushing the intercom button on her desk phone, she leaned toward the device, "Cheryl, bring in Jared's riding gear and his lunch."

Cheryl pushed a cart through the office door. Marta rose and picked up the leather jacket from the cart. Jared grabbed the sandwich in a plastic clam shell. "What's this?"

"Egg salad," Marta said while she held the jacket up in front of him.

"I prefer roast beef," Jared groaned as he pulled open the plastic clam shell.

"Put this on. I want to make sure it fits before you leave."

He shoved a chunk of the sandwich in his mouth and put the coat on. "Hmm, naah baf it."

Marta held the chaps up, then shoved them against his waist. "Hmm, when you get back you'll have to model—"

"NO." Jared set down the coffee cup that Cheryl had brought in. "I told you I'm not drinking anymore of that sugary coffee."

Draping the chaps over his shoulder, Marta nodded to Cheryl. "Take it back and bring him a cup of tea." Walking over to the couch, Marta sat down and crossed her legs. "Is that OK with you?"

He shook his head in agreement and took off the jacket.

Marta pointed her finger at the pile of leather on the floor. "Make sure those chaps fit. Along with the helmet."

He buckled the chaps' belt around his waist, then stuffed more of the sandwich into his mouth making sure to squish mustard onto his cheeks before facing Marta. "Wha' 'ou 'hink?"

She got up and grabbed a towel from her gym bag in the corner. Tossing it to him, she went to the door and closed it. "I have a project for you to do before you leave."

Wiping his face, he asked, "What is it?"

Coyly, she walked toward him unbuttoning her shirt. "Cowboy up. Nothing but the chaps."

Jared stood his ground. "No. I need to leave."

She grabbed his tanktop and pulled it down over his shoulders pinning his arms to his side. As he struggled to get his shirt back on, Marta undid his pants and let them drop. "If you're half as good as Kris says," she purred in his ear, "then the bike is yours when you get back."

"Kris?" Jared stopped fighting. "Mine?"

Marta undid her own pants and took them off. "The bike's all yours."

Chapter 22

Throwing the motorcycle gear in the car's trunk, Jared slammed the lid shut as Marta approached with a cup of coffee in her hand. He walked around to the driver's door and opened it.

Marta cooed as she handed him the cup, "Hurry back." As he took it she rubbed his crotch with her leg and pressed up against him. Purring, she whispered, "I can always use more of you."

Jared dropped onto the car seat in an effort to get away from her. "The bike'll be mine when I get back, right?"

"Depends. You'll have to come back in one piece and see me first."

Easing the car backwards to get her away from the door, Jared rolled the window down and stuck his head out. "I'll be back to collect what you promised me."

Out on the motorway, Jared turned the radio on and spun the dial. The static dissipated with the words: *Wicked Games by Chris Isaak, has moved up three places on the chart.* Jared turned the volume up and began to sing along with the song. When it came to the verse about losing someone like her, his eyes misted and he hammered the steering wheel with his fist. "Damn it, Angie. I never thought I'd lose you."

ANGELINA, IN HER FATHER'S dance studio, looked at herself in the mirror and listened to the same song as Jared was, playing on her radio. When the last note of the music faded, she wiped her face with both hands then turned away from her reflection. "Don't. He'll only break your heart." She walked out the studio door, heading across the plaza to the cathedral.

JARED WIPED HIS NOSE with his sleeve as another song started. Biting his lip, he grabbed the cup of coffee that Marta had given him. Taking a sip, he tasted its familiar bitter/sweet of her *special sugar*. He guzzled it down. The cup now empty, Jared looked around before tossing it out the window. As the miles flew by, the metallic after-taste in his mouth refused to go away. In desperation, he lit a cigarette; and then another.

Fully revved from the meth in the coffee, Jared drove all evening and late into the night. He stopped only for fuel, nothing else, hoping to make it a faster trip. All he could think of was to buy a new phone and call Angelina back.

After ten hours of nearly non-stop driving, his eyes began to blur with sleepiness. He was getting close to Brno and in an effort to stay awake, he shifted around while tapping his feet on the floor. It wasn't enough. He rolled the window down. Holding his head out, he spoke into the wind, "Hang on man, you can make it."

"I don't think I can."

Jared jerked his head back in at the sound of Danny's voice. Looking over at the passenger seat, he saw his dead friend with his good hand wrapped around the bloody stump of his blown off arm.

"It doesn't look good, does it, Sarge?"

"We'll make it, Danny," Jared bellowed, as he stomped on the accelerator.

"I'm cold Sa...Sa...arge. Tell my wife—"

"Shut up." Jared wiped his face with his arm. "We're gonna make it. Then you can tell her."

"Sarge... I can't feel my arm."

"Hang tight, Danny. We're gonna make it."

"I can't see my hand."

"Damn it, Danny, don't... "

"What's happening, Sarge? Everything's turning white..."

"Danny!" He reached over to comfort his friend, but all he could feel was the smooth leather of the seat.

Jared shuddered, then noticed the blue LED number on the speedometer; 186. His heart pounded as he lifted his foot off the gas and shot across the outer two lanes, aiming for an upcoming exit. He made it inside the dividing guardrail of the ramp, but not without losing the outside mirror. At the end of the ramp, he entered the roundabout with the speedometer still above 120. The car flew over the concrete center island. Jared managed to stop several blocks down the empty street on the other side.

He opened the door and rolled out onto the ground. Gasping for breath, he dry heaved a few times, then tried to spit the acrid taste from his mouth. Unable to, he crawled over to the car and climbed in. With the door open, he sucked in the cool night air in deep breaths. Slowly he turned his head and looked at the empty seat next to him. "Please God! Don't do this to me again. I tried to get him help." Tears rolling down his face, he beat on the steering wheel as he screamed, "It wasn't my fault. I tried... I tried... "

In the glow of approaching headlights, he wiped his face. As they got close, Jared reached out and pulled the door shut. After it had passed, he turned his car around and made his way back onto the motorway.

JARED PARKED THE CAR several blocks from the lot, then dialed the number. "Hello? I'm outside, open the gate." He flipped the phone closed and tossed it on the seat.

The guy at the gate whistled as the damaged car rolled by him. Pulling next to the garage, Jared popped the trunk and shut the engine off.

"What the hell'd you do to my car?" the manager yelled when he stepped out of the office.

Throwing his shirt in the trunk and putting on the leather coat, Jared spit on the ground. "You're lucky the thing didn't explode into little pieces."

"Just look at that mirror! I can't rent it like that."

Jared draped the chaps over his shoulder. "Not my problem." Grabbing the helmet and gloves, he slammed the trunk lid closed. "Where's the bike and my papers?"

"I'm not giving you anything." The manager knelt next to the wrinkled fender. "Not till I figure out how much damage you did to the car." He rose to his feet wiping his hands. "Looks like you're going to owe me."

Jared jumped in the manager's face. "I delivered the product. Nothing's touched it, it's still inside the car. So, give me the delivery papers."

He pushed Jared away. "Don't threaten me, you damn tweaker."

Throwing a sucker punch, Jared knocked the manager against the car and shoved his forearm against the man's throat. "Give me the flippin' envelope and the bike."

The gatekeeper stepped towards them.

Jared pointed a finger at him. "Bring 'em to me now! Or your boss here is gonna have some trouble breathing."

The guy looked at his boss; the manager nodded.

Jared stepped back, dropping his arm. "We both know what's hidden in the car is the real prize. I could care less what you people do with these cars, as long as I get my money."

"Somebody's going to pay for the car," the manager said as he massaged his throat. "And it won't be me."

Jared held out his hand and snapped his fingers. "Papers." The manager pulled an envelope from his breast pocket. Jared snatched it from his hand. "Not my problem," he said as he folded the brown envelope and shoved it inside his coat.

"I'd hate to be you, once Marta finds out how much damage you did to her car."

Straddling the bike, Jared glanced at the manager. "You're gonna tear it apart anyway. So what's the problem?"

"This is a car rental business not a chop-shop." The manager ran his finger along the deep scratch down the car's side.

"Whatever." Jared strapped on his helmet. "It doesn't matter to me what Marta does. She already has me on a payment plan."

Revving the motor, Jared didn't wait for a response. He popped the clutch and screamed out into the streets. In the middle of the night, he weaved through the light traffic in a hurry to get out of town before Marta called. After cutting it close and running several red lights, he noticed a car hanging back in the distance, keeping pace with him. It never got close, but made every turn and ran the lights, too in an effort to keep him in sight.

After making several circles, Jared found the on-ramp to the motorway. He cranked the throttle wide open and raced up the ramp. The car followed him. When the next exit came up, Jared waited until the last second then whipped over the white lines, down the single lane ramp to an intersection. He sat there watching the exit in his mirror.

The car slowed as it approached him. When the traffic light turned green, Jared pulled a hard left and screamed across the motorway overpass, then shut off his engine and lights, coasting down into a residential neighborhood.

He sat on the darkened street for twenty minutes before he quietly rode back to the motorway and headed away from the city in search of a fuel station.

Finding a small station at the end of a ramp, he pulled in, filled up and bought a cup of coffee. Outside, he sat on the curb drinking it as he smoked a cigarette. The flashing lights of a plane overhead made him think of Angelina.

"Dang. I forgot to buy a phone. Wait a minute, I wonder if her number's programmed in." Flipping open Marta's phone, he began to search the contents for its phone book. Before he could find it, the phone buzzed; it was Marta. Jared hit the answer button. "Yes?"

Where are you, Jared?"

"What? No hello?"

"Where's my motorcycle? You should be on the way."

"I believe the bike is mine and—"

"Don't play games with me. You should be on the motorway headed towards Prague, now."

Jared dropped the cigarette and glanced over at the motorway ramp. "I'm—" he noticed the car that had been following him sitting at the top of the ramp. "Gotta go. I'll call you back."

"No! Jared—"

Before he closed the phone, he held it up looking at the screen. The location symbol was illuminated. "Aww, that bitch. That's how she knew." He cocked his arm back to throw it away. "Nah, I may have a need for it." Popping the battery out, he shoved the disassembled phone in his coat and got on the bike. "Got a full tank of gas. Let's see if I can lose her friends on the scenic route home."

Jared kicked a brick loose from the planter beside him and placed it in his lap. Slowly cruising toward the on/off ramp, He turned the wrong way up the off ramp and picked up speed. The car sat there as he drove by, chucking the brick at their windshield.

Going against traffic, Jared rode on the inside shoulder until he spotted a gap in the median guardrail. Slipping through, he headed for the road to Vienna, in the opposite direction of Marta's demands.

THE POLIZEI STATION on the outskirts of Frankfurt looked the same as he remembered. Jared hid the bike in the shadows and went inside to see if the old jailer was still around. The old man was where he had left him six months earlier. When Jared knocked on the door frame, the old man put his pen down and rose, stretching out his hand. "Well, well, young man. How are you doing?"

Jared shook his hand. "I've got myself into a bind." He pointed at the chair next to the desk. "May I?"

The old man nodded as he closed the folder in front of him.

Unzipping his leather jacket, Jared pulled out his cigarettes. "I don't know who else to turn to." He held up the pack, offering one to the old man. The policeman declined as he shoved an ash tray across his desk.

Jared lit one for himself. "Anyway, I've fallen for this gypsy, but it seems her family has a side business that I've gotten myself entangled in, and..."

"You want out. Yes?"

"Yes...no. I mean I don't want to lose her, but—"

"If she is a gypsy like you say, then forget her. Among them, family ties are stronger than her love for you." The old man sat back and looked at the scowl on Jared's face. "What is it they do?" he asked. "I would hate to have several of my men go to the hospital if they happen to visit you again."

"Don't worry, you won't. I live in Amsterdam." Jared chuckled. " But I deliver cars for them, here in Frankfurt and few other cities in Germany." He snuffed out the cigarette. "That's why I'm here."

Entwining his fingers together over his stomach, the old man eyed Jared, then asked, "I take it we're talking more than cars being moved around?"

"At first I thought I was just returning cars back to the rental lots. Then, these last couple of cars..." the old man reached in a drawer and pulled out a file as Jared continued, "I realized there was more to it."

Opening the file, the policeman slid it in front of Jared.

Jared glanced at the photo. "That's not even my good side. You should have said something. I would have combed my hair."

"Interpol has been after that family for a long time." The policeman flipped the picture of Jared over. "I would hate to see you end up in a cage for her." He tapped a picture of Marta in an evening dress at a gala event, along with several famous people.

"If you're asking, I'm not going to squeal on anybody." Jared closed his eyes and massaged the bridge of his nose. "But, if you have a cup of coffee and a packet of sugar, I might be able to help."

The policeman nodded and stepped out of his office for the coffee. Jared pulled the empty brown envelope from his pocket and wrote on it; *try wetting the flap and tasting the sugar.*

The old man came in and set a cup of coffee in front of Jared, then placed a tray with several cubes of sugar next to it.

"I specifically asked for a packet of sugar."

"I'm sorry," he apologized, "but that's all we have." The old man spied the envelope and reached for it.

Jared quickly held the tray of sugar cubes down on top of the envelope so the policeman couldn't pick it up. "She always keeps packets of sugar in her desk drawer for the drivers." Unsure of what to do next, he reached for a cigarette and felt one of Marta's *special* packets still in his pocket. He took it out and waved it slowly for the old man to see. Forcing the contents to one end, then tearing the packet in two, he dropped half in the coffee, then set the other half under the sugar tray. Leaving the cup of coffee alone, Jared sat back and lit a cigarette.

The old man slowly brushed his bushy mustache as he watched the younger man.

"Last time we visited," Jared spoke up, "you asked me if I wanted to live my life this way. I don't. But...," his face went blank as he stared at the wall.

"But the demons won't leave you alone."

Jared fingered the shattered bullet pendent beneath his shirt. "They just keep coming back."

"I know how you feel, young man. Drugs and alcohol just encourage them to keep visiting." The old man opened a drawer in his desk retrieving a pendant. He rubbed it with his fingers. "I sat in your chair once." He set the St. Michael medallion on the desk and looked Jared in the eyes. "I found my faith in God kept them at bay far better than anything man made."

"That's nice." Jared rose to his feet and zipped his jacket. "I'm going home and grabbing a few things, then I'm going to disappear." He picked the medal up and read the prayer on the back. "Mind if I keep it?"

The policeman sat with his chin cradled in his hand as he watched Jared read it. He nodded.

"I'm also hoping," Jared pointed at the coffee, "that it will take your lab at least two days to figure things out."

The old man smiled. "It might take three... maybe four, just to be sure."

"Thank you." Jared reached in his coat pocket for the keys and felt the phone. "Oh," he pulled it out, "this belongs to Marta. Would you mind returning it?"

Chapter 23

In a small town outside of Frankfurt, he hid the bike between two cars. After picking up a cheap, non-traceable phone, he sat at a table at an outdoor cafe and called Hans. "Hey, Bud, it's me. Can we talk?"

"Jared! Marta has the family out looking for you. She's very angry with you!"

"You have to be kidding? All I did was scratch up one of her cars. Hang on a second, Hans..." Jared looked up at the waiter. "Coffee." The waiter nodded and left. "Hey, I need Angelina's number, my phone took a swim and quit working. Can I get her number from you?"

"Sorry, my friend. Marta has put a price on your head and I don't want my sister to get hurt."

"Over a scratched up car?"

"Is that your story? The people down in Bratislava say they found the car on the side of the road and the shipment was missing."

"Why that..." Jared slapped the table. "I dropped the car off at the lot. I even got the delivery papers."

"Even if you have papers, you are not safe. You understand my position, yes?"

"Yeah." Jared lit a cigarette and looked around. "But the least I can do is call your sister and explain to her—"

"She is mad at you, too. I don't think she will listen."

"How can I explain if I can't talk to her?" Jared nodded at the waiter as he set his coffee on the table. "How about an address so I can write to her?"

"Cannot do. Hey, I have to go. Customers are lining up and—"

"Wait! Hans. Can you at least go over to the house and pick up a few of my things?"

"Possibly. But then Marta will know you are here."

"I'll take that chance. All I want is my guitar, the photo of Angie, and my military papers. Ok?" Jared rubbed his cigarette out in the ashtray. "Put the papers and picture inside the guitar. And if anyone sees you, tell 'em you're taking the guitar because I owe you money."

"I don't know, Sarina said I cannot go in house."

"Get Olga to hand them to you out the back door."

"It won't be wise. Kris might see me."

"Then take it with you on the boat —"

"They'll be watching me," Hans protested.

"Play it while you wait for customers, you know how the game goes," Jared demanded. "Keep an eye on the bridges as you get close."

"And if I can't get it?"

Looking up at a plane flying over head, Jared insisted, "You can do it, my friend. I have faith in you."

PULLING UP TO THE HOTEL Valkren after dark, Jared chained his motorcycle to a tree, then quickly ran inside.

Shawn looked up from the book he was reading. "My friend. It's been a long time. How have you been?"

"Hey, Shawn." Jared held out his hand as he approached the counter. "I need a favor. Can I park my motorcycle in the garage?"

Shawn flipped his book closed. "It is for the customers, you know."

Jared scratched his unshaven face as he looked toward the door then laid two €100 notes on Shawn's book. "I need a place to stay for a few days."

"Ahh, problems with the gypsy girl." Shawn leaned back and looked under the counter. "I have one left, but it is up on the top floor and the bath is on the floor below."

"Fine. Can I get that motorcycle in the garage now?"

Shawn placed the room key on the counter. "Everything fine with your—"

Grabbing the key, Jared turned toward the door. "I'll tell you later. Right now I need to get that bike off the street."

Shawn slipped the money in his pocket. "No problem. I'll go unlock the door."

As the innkeeper swung the garage door closed and latched it, he looked at the bike Jared was shoving in the corner behind the hotel's van. "Fancy motorcycle. I see why you want to park it inside."

"There's more to it than that. I bought it from Marta, you know the sister to..." he pointed toward the cafe across the canal, "Sarina."

"Ja, ja. And?" Shawn knelt and looked at the motorcycle.

"Apparently one of Marta's associates ripped her off and fingered me as the one who did it." Setting his helmet on the bike, Jared shoved the ignition key in his pocket. "She has the whole clan out looking for me."

"Ohh, my friend. Didn't I warn you about getting involved with gypsies. Hey, what's this?"

"What's what?" Jared stepped around the bike.

The innkeeper reached under the fuel tank. "This does not belong here. It belongs on the—" Shawn squeezed the large rubber tube. "That is not right."

"What are you talking about? I just spent two days riding this thing, and there is nothing wrong with it."

"It is too ridged." Shawn twisted the questionable tubing and pulled it free.

"Way to go. I've had the bike two days, and now you've broken it."

Holding up the tube, Shawn stared into its end. "It is plugged with something. It never worked."

Jared grabbed the rubber tube from Shawn. "Huh, you're right," he said holding it up to the light. "There is something in there." Glancing around the garage, Jared spied a broom. "That should work."

Shawn held the broom handle as Jared slid the tube over it. Gently pushing on it, a brown, round paper package emerged.

"Whoa, the shipment they're looking for," Jared whispered as he pulled it free.

"There is something else," Shawn said as he pushed the broom further in.

Jared's face turned ashen as two more packages came out of the pipe. "Shi..., I'm screwed. They ain't gonna stop till I'm dead."

"You need to leave, my friend. Amsterdam is no longer safe for you."

"Pfft, to where? They have car lots in every country but Spain."

"Ahh, I would suggest you go there then. In the northwest corner. Where you could hide among the British ex-patriots."

"Yeah right, with all these drugs." He shoved two of the bundles in his coat pocket, then carefully tore the third one open. "Wow!" Jared whistled as he exposed a roll of money instead of drugs. "This changes everything." He unrolled and counted the American currency. "Fifty thousand! Yeow, a hundred fifty grand between the three! Now I know there's a bullet with my name on it."

Shawn ran his fingers through his hair. "Are you sure no one saw you come here?"

"I'm positive," Jared snapped. "Hey look, I'm gonna need your help. Hans is suppose to get a few things of mine from Marta's place and deliver them to me on one of the bridges."

"They'll be watching him," Shawn pointed out as he inspected the tube again.

Holding out the roll of cash in his hand, Jared asked, "Could you pick it up for me?"

Shawn stared at the money. "I'm... I—"

"Hey, take it. I owe you. Hide it from your wife and don't spend a cent for a month. By then Marta should be under wraps."

"What do you mean?"

Jared slapped the roll of cash in Shawn's hand. "With what happened back east and the missing money, she's bound to make a big mistake and get picked up."

Weighing the money in his hand, the innkeeper pondered out loud, "My customer's safety or.... It's a tough decision you have thrust on me, my friend." He shoved the roll in his jeans pocket. "What do you have in mind?"

With his arm around Shawn, Jared turned toward the stairway. "When Han's boat comes up the canal, you'll need to be drinking your coffee on the bridge. As he glides under, he'll slide a guitar onto the pavement next to your feet. Pick it up, go through the alley and at the other end, wait for me."

Chapter 24

With the sudden windfall of cash hidden in a money belt and his guitar on his back, Jared rode south towards Spain along the coastline. Stopping at a small gas station in Belgium, he bought a touristy city sticker to place on the bike.

The simple emblem changed the bike's image. Liking the idea, he stopped at each beach memorial in northern France and bought tourist stickers to put on the bike. By the time he got to the Pyrenees in Southern France, the motorcycle looked nothing like the sleek crotch rocket he had in Amsterdam.

Finally at France's border with Spain, Jared left the bike unchained outside the old custom's house while he went inside to buy a toll sticker. Gone for only ten minutes, he stepped out in time to catch a thief trying to break the bike's ignition lock.

"Hey you," Jared yelled, as he ran toward the motorcycle.

The thief jumped off and ran towards a waiting van. He leaped into its open side door and the van took off, spinning its tires.

As he reached his bike, Jared managed to make out the first three letters on the van's plate before it disappeared around the corner.

"Gees, I can't believe it. Can't leave anything for a minute and someone tries to steal it."

He started the motor and let it idle while he peeled the back off the toll sticker. After placing it among the other stickers on the bike's fender, he rode off into Spain.

Thrilled with the beauty of the road, along with the vistas, Jared held his speed down while he cruised the curvy highway. Occasionally he would hear the high pitched whine of other motorcycles as they raced up behind him and then passed by in a blur of speed. Often they were followed by a sports car trying to keep up.

The mountainous road seemed to go on forever with no rest stops. Cresting a hill, Jared came upon a wide graveled shoulder and pulled off. Leaving the bike idling, he jumped off and walked onto the grass at the edge of the gravel to relieve himself. Done, and making an effort to zip his pants with his gloved hands, he heard the bike rev. Turning, he saw a leather-jacketed thief straddling the bike, put it in gear and pop the clutch. It killed the motor. Jared dropped his guitar from his back and ran toward the bike.

The thief quickly got it started again, down shifted, and dropped the clutch once more, spraying Jared with gravel as he reached for the guy. Covering his face with his arms to protect himself, Jared stumbled and fell. He lie in the gravel and watched the bike disappear over the hill, followed by the same van that had tried to steal it the first time.

"Damn," he groaned standing up. "I should have known better."

Kicking at the gravel, he walked back and picked up his guitar. With the strap over his shoulders, he walked along the road. About a mile down the road a rest stop came into sight. "Wouldn't ya know," he swore and pulled a cigarette out. "Let's just hope that wasn't Marta's repo men in the van and they're waiting here for me."

From the edge of the parking lot, Jared stared at all the parked cars to see if the van was there. There wasn't a single van. He felt safe enough then to go to the cafe entrance. "Always wondered if that bike had a locator hidden on it," he pondered as he held the door open. After one last scan of the lot, Jared stepped inside mumbling to himself, "Kinda glad it's gone. Cause if it did, she can't trace me now."

Inside the door, a picture of snow-covered mountains with a small bus in the lower corner advertising a local tour package, greeted him.

Jared looked around the cafe/store. There were several more tour advertisements on chrome stands placed in the aisles. He stepped in line for the cashier and tried reading the posters while he waited.

When it was his turn the clerk looked at Jared and asked, "*Si?*"

Jared looked at one of the signs and laid a €50 on the counter. "El bus-o to ahh... San Sebastian. Ahh... uno way."

"We don't sell bus tickets here." The clerk then pointed at a desk in the corner. "They do, but they're closed now. You'll have to come back in the morning."

Picking up the cash, Jared rolled his eyes. "Just my luck. Thank you."

A man waiting in line motioned to Jared as he stepped from the counter. "I'm going to San Sebastian, delivering a load of manure. I could use someone to talk to on the way."

"Thank you." Jared nodded and shoved the cash in his pocket.

The trucker raised his eyebrows, cocked his head and held out his hand. "Fuel is expensive."

"So is losing a bike," Jared groaned. He pulled the cash out, looked at it, then slapped it in the guy's hand.

Stepping up to the counter, the trucker shoved his card into the card reader. "Bandits got your bike, eh? So far, I've been lucky with this load."

Jared winced at the thought. "Who would steal a truck load of manure?"

The driver put his card back in his pocket, then put a finger to his lips. "Fertilizer has many uses. And there are just as many people who would steal it."

"No problem. I've ridden shotgun on more dangerous roads than this." Jared unzipped his leather motorcycle jacket and stretched his neck. "If you get us there before the bars close, I'll buy you a beer."

"You've got yourself a deal. Let's go."

ON THE OUTSKIRTS OF San Sebastian, the trucker turned into the parking lot of a low-slung warehouse and parked his rig. "Come on," he said as he climbed out. "I believe you owe me a beer."

Walking around in front of the truck with his guitar and helmet in hand, Jared asked, "We walking or you calling a cab?"

"There's a hotel about ten minutes outside the gate. We can drop our things there, then go to a little bar around the corner from it. Great place, but it can get a bit noisy when the dancers start stomping."

"Don't tell me you found an Irish pub here in Spain," Jared joked at the thought.

"I wish, laddy. No, they do some kind of Spanish dance, like they're trying to put out a fire. I go there 'cause the food's good and the beer is cold."

Hoisting his guitar onto his back, Jared laughed. "It's called flamenco, and the only reason you go there is because it's cheap."

"Quiet, lad. You sound like my wife." The trucker bumped Jared's arm and whispered, "In reality, the gypsies that run the bar are very beautiful."

"Gypsies?" Jared stopped at the crosswalk with his toes hanging over the edge of the curb. "Is this a private club?"

"Nah." The driver bellowed at Jared from the middle of the crosswalk, "If you have a problem with gypsies, lad, you've came to the wrong place. Basque country is full of them."

Sucking in a deep breath of night air, Jared looked down the street and followed. "I don't. But there's a few up north that would like to get hold of me."

The trucker switched hands on his bag. "You got caught with one of their girls? Ha, ha, and the family wants your head, yes?"

"You might say that's it, in a nutshell."

"Well your in luck, lad." He slapped Jared on the back. "The Basque barely tolerate the clans from up north. Myself, I avoid them too, but let's just say you're reasonably safe down here."

"I was hoping that would be the case." Jared reached for the hotel door and held it open. "Looks respectable."

"What?" the trucker asked as he stepped past Jared.

"I said, better than sleeping under a bridge."

Chapter 25

"Angelina... Angelina." Her father leaned forward and tapped her arm. "I'm over here. You need to face me so I can hear you."

She twisted around."Sorry, father." Leaning back in the wire mesh cafe chair, she sipped her coffee. "It's just that, that man in the middle of the square playing his guitar, looks like Jared."

"I thought you were over him." He set his cup down and put on his glasses. Looking at the man she was talking about, he asked, "Should we go talk to him?"

"No!" Angelina snarled.

"Didn't you say he was a good dancer? And that you enjoyed his company?"

"He is. And yes I did." She set her cup down and gave the troubadour another fleeting glance. "But I'm not going to compete with cars for his attention."

Her father took off his glasses and folded them into his pocket. "You would rather compete against women like Marta and Kris?"

"Papa!" She folded her arms and slumped back into her chair. "I don't ever want to hear those names again." Biting her thumbnail, she whimpered, "It's not fair."

"Life's not fair, my child. That is why we go to church and pray for intercession—"

Angelina reached out and smacked the table. "I did that. And look what happened."

He grabbed her hand. "Angelina. Your mother prayed every day for my return from Afghanistan."

"I remember." Angelina gently pulled her hand away. "And we..." she thumped her chest, "me and Hans that is, paid for it."

"I know, I'm sorry. Had I known about the committee's purge, I would have abandoned my post and come home sooner."

"That would have made us orphans." Angelina rose to her feet. "I know you did what you could."

Her father rose and stepped around the table, giving her a hug. "I didn't do enough."

She hugged him back, then stepped away. Looking down at the cobblestone under their feet, she whispered, "I have to go and get the classroom ready."

"I'll be there after I finish my coffee." He sat down and watched her walk away. Only to have his thoughts interrupted by his phone buzzing. "Da?"

"This is Stefon," a voice said. "The answer to you inquiry, is yes."

"Are you sure?"

"I talked to her myself."

"OK, balshoye spaseeba."

Ordering two cups of coffee to go, he turned and watched the young man in the plaza until the coffee arrived. Sauntering across the square, Angelina's father listened to the song that the young man was singing. He stopped in front of the street performer and set one of the cups next to the musician's guitar case.

With the last note, Jared let the strings continue to resonate while he used his sleeve to wipe his eyes.

"You play very well. What is the name of that one?"

"*Prisoner*, by Joe Bonamassa." Jared pointed at the cup of coffee placed next to his guitar case. "Is that for me?"

"That depends... can you play me something that sounds similar to Enrique?"

"Uuh, that name sounds familiar... I'm not sure, though." Jared plucked the strings of his guitar one at a time. "A friend in Amsterdam taught me this one. I never heard him play it at any of the dances, though." Jared began to play the one Spanish flamenco song that Hans had taught him.

Angelina's father smiled. "Excellent, excellent. You have very gifted fingers my friend. He picked up the cup and held it out to Jared. "Are you looking for someone, or just passing through?"

"That depends." Jared took a sip of the coffee. "I'm looking for someone. And if I find her, then I'm staying. What about you?"

"I have a studio close by, where I can tinker about. But with this..." he held up his three-fingered left hand, "it's a challenge to play the music I love. "

Jared slipped his guitar into its case. "Sorry to hear that."

"So you're looking for a woman, yes?" Angelina's father asked.

Jared stood up. "What?"

"Forgive me, I did not mean to change the topic." He pointed towards the empty table he had left earlier. "Shall we sit and talk? I would like to hear some more of your music."

"Hmm." Jared scratched his forehead. "I don't really need the conversation, but I could use something to eat."

"Please, let us sit and discuss music while I buy you something to eat."

"Yeah. Sure. Why not." Jared slipped the case onto his back.

"I was hoping you'd say that." Her father held out his arm toward the cafe. "Shall we?"

Walking toward the table, Angelina's father gazed across the plaza at the cathedral, then at Jared. "Now, I must warn you, it can get a bit noisy in a few moments."

"From what? The pigeons?" Jared snickered.

With a serious look on his face, he placed his hand on Jared's chest and looked him in the eyes. "The bells," he warned, then continued to walk towards the cafe.

Jared hopped over a soccer ball rolling across his path. "You're joking?"

"Possibly." He touched Jared's arm. "There is one thing you must promise me when you leave. You will forget all about this place."

Choking on the coffee in his mouth, Jared wiped his face. "Look, Mister..." he waved the cup in front of Angelina's father.

"Sokolov."

"Mister Sokolov, I've been through a lot in my life. I think I can decide for myself what to do."

"So I've been told," Sokolov whispered as he sat. "But, she is special to me, too."

"I know some people have an affinity for keeping things the way they are." Jared propped his guitar against the table. "But the girl I'm looking for means a lot to me."

Sokolov waved his hand at the waiter. "Why did she leave, if you don't mind me asking?"

"Family problems."

"Oh? Yours or hers?" Sokolov asked as the waiter set a basket of bread on the table between them. Looking up at the waiter, he pointed at their cups. "Two more, please."

"Hers... me... I don't know. Every time I tried to talk to her, we got interrupted." Jared reached for a breadstick. "I don't know... I don't want to lose her, but I don't want to... ." He looked at Sokolov. "Sorry, didn't mean to ramble on about myself."

"It's quite alright." Pulling out a pack of cigarettes, he took one and placed the others on the table. "Cigarette?"

"Thank you." Jared glanced at the pack as he picked it up. When he saw the brand, he shuddered. "I haven't seen this kind in a while."

"Oh? You've been to the Ukraine?"

Jared took one from the pack and gently fingered the cigarette before sliding it under his nose, inhaling its scent. "No, saw them in Kabul, Afghanistan."

"Tourist shop?"

Poking the paper-tube holder between his lips, he shook his head and leaned back, struggling to dig out his lighter.

Sokolov slid his own etched chrome lighter across the table.

Abandoning his effort, Jared picked up Sokolov's lighter. He saw the picture of a Soviet T-66 and went numb. He sat there staring through the lighter's flame, out into the plaza.

Danny, with his one arm, was standing in the middle of the square, going through the motions of rock, paper, scissors. Blinking, Jared looked away and saw Dave flipping a coin over and over.

Angelina's father snapped his fingers in front of Jared.

"Sorry," Jared shook his head, "my friend Dave had one like this." He lit his cigarette, then gently closed the lid and handed the lighter back. "I didn't mean to drift off."

"What happened to him? Your friend?"

His eyes misting up, Jared sniffed and looked across to the far side of the plaza. "He didn't make it."

"I'm sorry to hear that." Sokolov held up the lighter and glanced at both its sides before putting it away. "I've been where you are, my friend." He took a sip of his coffee and followed Jared's stare out into the plaza. "I can see, Jared, you're afraid of the demons that still haunt you. That they might kill anyone you get close to. You need to decide who's in charge of your life. God, or your demons."

Jared glared at Angelina's father, "How'd you know my name? Did Marta send you after me?"

Sokolov pulled a piece of bread apart and pointed, "I assume that is your name on your guitar case, yes?"

Jared nodded.

"You can't ignore the demons, but you can get help controlling them and putting them in the past." He laid the rest of the breadstick down and wiped his mouth.

"That's what they say, but I ain't taking any of that chemical crap. It'll kill you." Jared stood up. "I think I took enough of your time."

Sokolov pointed at Jared's chair. "Please sit. We're not finished."

"What makes you think so?"

"Because I know who you're looking for, and we need to discuss that."

Jared slid back into his chair. "You know where Angelina is staying?"

"Yes. And she doesn't want to see you anymore. I also suggest you don't try to find her."

"Who the hell are you to tell me, what—"

"I'm her father."

"I want... oh." Taking a deep breath, he looked at Sokolov. "I mean, your daughter gave me meaning. Not in the sense like the Army did. More so. You know what I mean?"

Watching the smoke from his own cigarette curl upward and drift away, Sokolov nodded. "Her mother was my anchor the first time I returned from war." He deeply inhaled through his nose. "The secret police killed her before I could get home the second time. It wasn't until I drank myself into a morass of self pity and was about to lose my children, did I reach out to God. He can save you from the self-doubt, the torment of the visitations."

"So if I don't agree with you, you're not gonna—"

Sokolov picked up his lighter, flicked it open and lit it. He held it up and let the flame burn until Jared stopped talking and sat back. He blew out the flame then went on to say, "Marta has a bounty on you, a sizable one at that. And I'm not going to risk Angelina's life for your happiness."

"I'll take her to America with me. We'll be safe there. Marta would never find us."

"I would like to see my daughter go there some day." He flicked the lighter closed. "But the answer is still no."

"What?"

"Young man, we both have been in battle. Because of my struggle to cope, she paid dearly while growing up."

Jared tossed the paper tube filter leftover from the cigarette onto the metal table. "I told you, I'm going to be OK. I haven't had a problem in..."

Sokolov laid his lighter on the table with the image of the tank facing up. Jared glanced away.

"Unfortunately son, you have not yet come to terms with the death of your friends. I will not put her through that again."

Draining his cup, Jared looked at a man in the middle of the plaza setting up a paint easel, and then at the cup in his own hand. "Before I can agree, I'd like to hear it from her."

Sokolov rose to his feet and placed a handful of coins next to his cup. "By all means. I think you should."

Chapter 26

Following Sokolov into his studio, Jared glanced around the large room at the odd assortment of decorations on the wall. Crossed swords, cow horns, a painting of a matador. On another wall was one of a gypsy caravan, next to a pair of ballet slippers. Then there was a large mural of a field of yellow sunflowers.

Walking past the upright piano next to the stage, Jared caught a whiff of a familiar scent. He stopped and closed his eyes, taking in a deep breath.

Sokolov opened a door into an anteroom. "This is..." he turned and saw Jared motionless with his eyes closed. "Is there a problem?"

"No, no." Jared opened his eyes. "The piano reminded me of her. So, what were you going to say?" He strode over to where Sokolov stood.

"You need to wait out here."

"Who you talking to, Father?" Angelina's voice asked from upstairs.

Excited at hearing her voice, Jared opened his mouth to speak.

Sokolov held his hand up in Jared's face, then leaned through the doorway. "Come down, my dear, there is someone here to talk to you."

"But I—" Jared protested.

"She is my daughter," Sokolov cut him short. "Follow me." He placed his hand on Jared's arm.

Reluctant, Jared glanced at the door. "I want to—"

"I know what you want." He gripped Jared's arm tighter. "And I know what she wants."

"Whoa." Digging in his heels, Jared pulled his arm free. "Not this time."

Sokolov glared at him like only a hardened military officer could. "You'll do as I say."

"Yes, sir."

He lead Jared over to the piano. "Here, sit."

"But..."

"But nothing, young man. Don't think I can't defend my house."

"Yes, sir."

The door opened and Angelina stepped into the room. Her face went blank. "Father! How could you?" she yelled and marched toward him. He held a finger to his lips, then motioned her to come beside him.

"How could you?" she mouthed as she stepped next to her father.

Sokolov stood brushing his mustache. "He has something to ask you."

Sighing, Angelina turned around, bumping against Jared who had stood up behind her. "What is it you want?"

"To speak to you. I've been trying to apologize for over two weeks now, and every time I start, someone steps between us."

She tried to side-step around him. "I don't have time for this."

Jared got in her way. "Which is it? You don't want me around, or you don't want to admit you were wrong?"

"I..." she glanced up into his eyes, "I..."

He put his finger on her lips. "You told me Marta was dangerous and I didn't listen. That was my fault. Not yours." He gingerly took hold of her hand and raising it to his lips, kissed it. "I'm sorry. I should have listened, but I needed the money... for us."

Angelina pulled her hand away. "You not having money was never a concern with me, but it was to Kris. By the way, how is my sweet little cousin?"

Jared closed his eyes, then slowly opened them looking at her. "A pain in my backside. It's you that I need, not her. You make my life complete. I need you."

"No, Jared. You don't need me." Angelina stepped back away from him. "I was using you."

"What are you talking about?"

"I used you. My brother used you. Marta used you." Angelina turned her head away as a tear rolled down her cheek.

"What are you saying?" Jared gently pulled her face back around. "Are you saying you didn't love me? That it was fake?"

Tears streaming down her face, she nodded.

"I don't believe you." He kissed her hand. "I'll love you till I die."

She shook her head. "No. No, you need to forget me." She pulled her hand away. "Go home. You'll forget me in time." She turned and ran up the stairs.

Her father grabbed Jared's arm before he could run after her. "Let's step outside, son."

Holding back his emotions, Jared took a deep breath, and nodded, before following him out.

Outside, Sokolov took out his Zippo and lit Jared's cigarette, then flicked the lighter closed, and then open, and then closed. "Satisfied?"

"No, but—"

Open... closed...open...closed, the clicking sound of the lighter interrupted Jared for a moment.

"Sir, I love your daughter, but—"

Open...closed...open...closed.

Jared lowered his eyes with the sound from the lighter echoing in his ears and stared at the sidewalk.

Open...closed...open.

In an effort to ignore the controlling, clicking sound, he raised his eyes and gazed past Sokolov out into the plaza. Dave, still flipping a coin over and over, stood next to Danny, who was holding his good arm out motioning for Jared to come with them.

"Jared!" Sokolov snapped his lighter closed, gripping it in his fist, "You need to go home where you'll be safe, and can forget about Angelina."

Wiping tears from his eyes, Jared nodded his head with the obedience of a soldier and walked across the plaza toward the train station.

BACK IN THE SMALL TOWN where he had grown up in, Jared's sister got a call from the VA. They said Jared had fallen from a window and that she needed to come right away. It was a two hour drive to the VA hospital and having made this trip several times, helping Jared as he floundered through their treatment program for PTSD, she switched on the radio to ease her mind.

George Jones's voice wailed from the speakers singing the song, *He Stopped Loving Her Today*. As she listened to the words, she glanced at the little Flamenco dancer stuck to the dashboard of her car. Jared had glued it there on one of those trips to the hospital as he rambled about Angelina and the "Dear John" letter she had sent him months before. George's song was of a man's tortured and undying love for the woman who had spurned him, finally ended with his death. Wiping her nose on her sleeve, she knew Jared was finally at peace.